PLAY THE PART

Road Trip
romance

A.K. EVANS

This is a work of fiction. Names, characters, places, and incidents are the product of the author's imagination or are used fictitiously. Any resemblance to actual events, locales, or persons, living or dead, is coincidental.

Cover Artist
cover artwork © Sarah Hansen, Okay Creations
www.okaycreations.com

Editing & Proofreading
Ellie McLove, My Brother's Editor
www.grayinkonline.com

Formatting
Stacey Blake at Champagne Book Design
www.champagnebookdesign.com

PLAY THE
PART

CHAPTER 1

Cora

"I DON'T CARE WHAT IT COSTS. YOU HAVE TO DO THIS FOR me, Cora."

I often wondered what goes through the minds of people with extreme wealth. What makes them do the things they do? What lengths will they go to in any situation to benefit themselves?

On some level, I've found it fascinating to consider the answers to those questions. But mostly, I end up finding that I'm irritated by what it almost always seems to come down to.

Entitlement.

And I know that's not truly the case in every situation. In fact, I believe there are tons of wealthy individuals out there who really do work hard to achieve their success without needing to stomp on the little guy to do it.

Unfortunately, I haven't met any of them.

In my line of work, I wasn't sure I ever would either.

No, that's not right.

I was absolutely certain I wouldn't.

Even still, I'd continue to work for people like Priscilla, the only daughter of one of New York's most notably wealthy powerhouse couples. The woman who came from wealth and was marrying into wealth, though not as much as her family had.

She hadn't worked a day in her life.

And she never would.

Nope. She was born into a life that meant she could do anything she wanted with herself, but she chose to play the part of the spoiled, rich girl. It didn't necessarily bother me that she chose not to make something of herself. I just couldn't understand why she wouldn't want to. Surely, with the amount of wealth her family had, Priscilla had every opportunity available to her. There wasn't anything she couldn't have had access to because her father gave her everything.

I knew that for a fact.

Because he was giving her this wedding.

The wedding for which she was paying me to be a professional bridesmaid.

I was shocked years ago when I was considering becoming an event planner that such a thing even existed.

But it did.

And in a city like Manhattan, there was no shortage of business.

So, I took my event planning idea a step further and put my focus on becoming a professional bridesmaid. That title can mean different things to different individuals, but for me, it means that I basically do everything to fulfill the role of a legitimate bridesmaid without actually being in the wedding.

There are some in this line of business who will stand in at a wedding if the bride asks, but I've made it a strict rule not to do that. It just gets messy, and there are too many other things I am typically dealing with on the wedding day. The last thing I need to worry about when I'm trying to do my job properly is whether I've got the right bra on for the dress I'll need to wear or if the shoes are going to kill my feet.

For these reasons and then some, I stick to handling all the behind-the-scenes action. I do everything the real bridesmaids are supposed to do. It allows them to enjoy the day properly with the bride while I do all of the heavy lifting.

Sometimes it's the literal heavy lifting, too. I once had a bride whose dress weighed twenty-five pounds. While that might not seem like a lot, when the bride needed to relieve herself, she realized just how bad of an idea her dress had been. So, someone had to help her. That someone was me.

And I loved it.

Truly, I adored my job.

I enjoy planning, organizing, and being in control of what is typically a very chaotic day for a lot of couples and their families. I still do love that part of my job. But for the last year or so, I've just felt bitterness. And it's only ever been when I've dealt with clients who were extraordinarily wealthy.

I knew why.

My reasons might have been personal, but I knew enough to know I couldn't allow them to affect the job I did. Ever since I started feeling this way, I'd managed to do that. This was mostly because I hadn't really had any major situations arise that would cause those emotions to resurface.

So, the fact that I currently had Priscilla standing in front of me demanding I do something for her that I've had a strict rule about since I officially shifted the focus of my business years ago to being a professional bridesmaid had me feeling less than pleasant.

But I was doing my best to remain in control of my emotions.

"You know I have a policy in place for that, Priscilla," I started, my voice kind. I tried to sound as understanding and compassionate as I could when I continued, "But perhaps we can sit down and try to come up with another solution."

"There's no way, Cora!" she objected. "My pictures are going to be ruined if you don't stand in."

I took in a deep breath.

Priscilla was getting married in less than twenty-four hours. One of her eight bridesmaids had just been rushed to the hospital to have an emergency appendectomy. The doctors said there was no way she'd be able to make it to the wedding. As a result, Priscilla needed a last-minute bridesmaid and wanted me to step up to the plate.

"Are you certain there isn't anyone else you can ask that would be willing to stand in for you tomorrow?" I asked. "Surely, you'd rather have someone who's a friend or family member anyway."

She shook her head. "I have two other people I can ask, but neither one of them will fit in the dress. You will. *Please*, Cora, I'm begging you. I already talked to my dad and Sebastian. Both of them are willing to pay you. Whatever it's going to take to convince you to stand in tomorrow."

"Priscilla—" I began. Before I could get another word out, she cut me off.

"We'll add ten thousand dollars on top of what you're already billing for the wedding," she blurted. "I'm desperate."

Just like that.

Like it was nothing, she was willing to spend her father's and her soon-to-be husband's money. And she was willing to do it for the perfect picture wedding.

Someone like Priscilla was used to getting her way. If I fought her on this, she'd keep pushing. She'd do it because she was desperate, sure. But she'd also do it because she knew she could. Because whenever something happened in her life that needed to be fixed, money would always be there to handle her problems.

Realizing I was gearing up for a losing battle if I continued to deny my client, I finally huffed, "Fine. I'll do it. But I'm not going to get my hair done at some fancy place that'll kill my scalp with three hundred bobby pins."

Jumping up out of her seat, Priscilla squealed and clapped her hands. "You're the best!" she exclaimed.

Yep.

That was me.

I was the best.

I stood and rounded my desk as Priscilla came toward me. She threw her arms around me, hugged me, and promised, "You're going to have such a great time."

"I'm going to be working," I reminded her.

"Yeah, yeah," she brushed me off. "Earlier in the day, of course. But once we get to the reception, I'm sure it's all going to be smooth sailing. After all, I have no doubts you've already gone ahead and called to make sure everyone's doing everything they're supposed to be doing so that the day is a success."

If nothing else, she was at least right about that. No matter who it was, I took my job very seriously. Rich client or not, I expected them to get the very best of what they paid for, so I always saw to it that things were handled ahead of time in order to make sure we avoided any wedding-day disasters. And in all my years of doing this, I hadn't had any major debacles. There were only a few small unexpected and unfortunate situations that had arisen during the last couple of years, but none of it was anything catastrophic.

"So, the rules are that you'll do what needs to be done in the morning to make sure I can get married to the man of my dreams without a hitch. But once the party starts, I want you to join in on the fun. You deserve that for stepping up and doing this for me. Thank you, Cora."

I returned a smile and said, "You're welcome, Priscilla."

She turned to walk away when suddenly she stopped, looked back, and gave me her wide eyes.

"What?" I asked, worried that she suddenly had another problem.

My concerns dissipated immediately when she started grinning. But once she spoke, I felt nothing but dread. "I just realized you'll be paired up with Ben tomorrow," she explained. "If anyone can make sure you have a good night, it's him."

She didn't give me a chance to respond because the next thing I knew I was standing there alone in my tiny New York City office dreading what tomorrow would bring. Not an ounce of it had to do with anything pertaining to the wedding. It was all about him.

Benjamin Mason.

The worst possible thing that could have happened to me.

I stood there, unmoving, for longer than I would have under any other circumstances. It was a good thing Priscilla had offered a ten-thousand-dollar bonus for what I was going to be doing tomorrow because there wasn't any doubt in my mind that I was going to earn every single cent of it.

I hadn't ever expected that I'd develop the skills that would allow me to double as a seamstress, but my job required it. In every case prior to today, though, it had always been needed in order to fix something minor on the bride's gown, a bridesmaid dress, or even the occasional mother-of-the-bride dress.

Never.

Not once have I ever needed to utilize my sewing skills on a workday for something I was wearing. Unfortunately, since I'd stupidly agreed to stand beside Priscilla and fill in for her bridesmaid, I needed to make some adjustments to the gown. It was just a touch too long for me, and I needed to adjust the straps.

It had been more than five minutes since I'd completed that task when my phone rang.

"Hello?" I answered.

"Hi, Cora. It's Sebastian. Priscilla just called me frantic and panicking," he shared.

Sebastian was Priscilla's soon-to-be husband. If he was calling, I could only imagine the horror of what was happening.

"I'm getting ready to head over and meet her and the rest of the bridal party. I should be at the venue within the next thirty minutes or so. What's going on?"

"Apparently, she just spoke with the owner of the bake shop," he said.

That was odd. I was their point of contact for everything. "Really? Why would they call her?" I asked.

"I have no idea," he started. "Honestly, I don't know if they reached out to her or if it was the other way around. Regardless, there was a problem with one of their delivery vehicles, and now it's stranded."

"Are you serious?"

"I wish I were joking," he mumbled. "Anyway,

apparently the vehicle that was carrying the cake left earlier this morning and has already delivered the cake, but this one had all the extra desserts. They're not sure if they'll be able to get another delivery truck rerouted and back to the stranded one. I called my cousin to head over to meet the driver and let him know that I'd be calling you. Ben would make sure everything got to the venue, but he's not going to be able to fit all of it into his car. Would you be able to meet him?"

This couldn't really be happening. It would be my luck that I'd have to meet Ben, of all people, to deal with this catastrophe. Normally, I would have welcomed the help from extended family members. More often than not, they helped to lighten the mood in what were typically stressful situations.

Taking in a deep breath, I asked, "Where do I need to meet them?"

Sebastian rattled off the location, and I learned that this whole debacle just went from bad to worse. Traffic would be a nightmare.

The delivery truck broke down on a one-way street. It was probably a safe assumption that he was stuck in the middle of the road with the drivers of cars honking at him as they angrily drove by.

"I'll take care of it," I assured the groom.

After we disconnected, I threw the dress on a hanger, put it in a garment bag, and grabbed the remainder of my things. Then, I dashed out the door of my rent-controlled apartment and down to my car.

In any other situation, I wouldn't have lived in New

York City and owned a car. I lived here not only because it made sense for my business, but also because I was fortunate enough to have a rent-controlled apartment. Otherwise, there was no way I'd be able to afford living in a city like this.

And the car was a necessity for my job. I needed to be able to come to the rescue when a situation arose, a situation such as this one.

Once I was on my way, I connected to the Bluetooth and called Priscilla. It rang once before she answered, "Cora! Did Sebastian call you about the desserts?"

"Yes, Priscilla, he did. I'm on my way to take care of it now. Once I get that dealt with, I'll be there to meet you and the rest of the girls. I'll just need to get this dress and shoes on," I told her.

"What about pictures?" she asked, clearly beginning to fret.

"Don't worry about pictures," I ordered. "I'll be there with plenty of time to spare. We're good. Just relax and get yourself ready."

I disconnected with her and weaved my way through New York City traffic. That had been another art I'd perfected over the years. While it wasn't my favorite thing to do, it was necessary. And I was the kind of girl that if I was going to do something, I was going to do it right. So, even though I grew up in a suburb roughly two hours outside of the city, it wasn't long before I joined the ranks of city drivers and drove fearlessly.

I managed to arrive on the street the truck was on, but I still needed to travel three blocks to get to it. While

I waited in the barely-moving traffic, I glanced at the clock. There was still enough time to handle this and get to Priscilla before they were scheduled to start pictures.

Ten minutes later, I'd pulled up behind the truck and threw on my hazards. Sure enough, there was just a constant stream of honking horns as the cars pushed past us. I managed to climb across the center console to the passenger seat so I could get out on the side opposite of the angry drivers.

"Hi, Miss," the driver said as I approached.

"Hi," I greeted him. "I'm Cora."

"Roberto," he returned.

Giving him a nod, I asked, "Can you help me get these in the back of my car so I can get over to the venue?"

"Yes. I'm so sorry about this," he lamented.

"It's okay," I assured him. "Stuff happens."

Suddenly, I heard a deep voice rumble behind me, "That's all I can fit. The rest will have to go with whoever they're sending for it."

Slowly, I turned around and looked up at him.

Benjamin Mason.

One of New York City's most eligible bachelors.

His eyes were covered by sunglasses, but I could tell he'd shifted his gaze from Roberto to me.

"That would be me," I informed him.

"Who are you?" he asked after a beat of silence.

That figured. Ben and I were both at the wedding rehearsal a couple days ago. I, of course, did what I had gone there to do, but he was so distracted on his phone

11

that I wasn't surprised he didn't recognize me as a familiar face.

"Cora Daniels," I introduced myself, extending my hand to him.

His head shifted toward my hand, back to my face, and down to my hand again before he engulfed my hand in his.

"Ben Mason," he stated.

As if I didn't already know.

"Nice to meet you," I forced out in an attempt to be cordial.

I tried to pull my hand from his, but he had a firm grip on it. It wasn't until Roberto chimed in, "Okay, Miss, I've got the first batch here. Do you want to take these while I get another batch?"

I used Roberto's interruption and the distraction it offered to Ben so I could yank my hand away. "Yes," I declared. "I'll take them."

I reached to take the boxes of desserts from Roberto before I walked to the back of my car. Once there, I realized I should have opened the back gate because now my hands were full and I couldn't.

"Let me get that for you," Ben offered.

Okay, so maybe he wasn't a complete jerk. Though, I guessed it was unfair of me to make that assumption. It was just that I'd had enough experience with people like him.

"Thank you," I returned as I put the boxes inside.

By that point, Roberto had arrived with another stack. I took them from him and put them next to the ones I'd already situated inside. When I looked up again, Ben had a couple boxes in his hands.

Color me impressed.

Either he was legitimately a decent guy, or perhaps he just really cared about his cousin.

Ben didn't hand the boxes to me. Instead, he placed them inside my car with the others. Before I could say anything, Roberto was back and declared, "Here's the last of them."

"Perfect. Thank you so much."

"You're welcome. Again, I'm so sorry about all of this," he apologized for a second time.

"It's okay, but I've really got to get going," I returned.

He gave me a nod and moved back toward his truck. I closed the door on the back of my SUV and turned to Ben. "Thanks for helping me get these loaded up. Did you want me to take the ones you have in your car?"

Ben shook his head. "Don't worry about it. I'll get them over there."

"Are you sure?" I asked.

I didn't want to risk everything not being taken care of.

"Positive."

"Okay, then. I've got to get going."

He took a step toward me as he grinned.

I didn't know why he was giving me the look he was, but it freaked me out. I took two steps backward, and the next thing I knew, a horn was blaring as Ben reached out and pulled me toward him. The car had zipped by, narrowly missing me.

13

"Oh my God," I breathed in shock.

"Are you okay?" Ben asked, his voice full of concern.

That's when I took a brief moment to evaluate the situation. My body was plastered to Ben's, and he was holding me tight. I normally wouldn't have thought anything of it considering what had just happened, but I was finding that I liked how it felt. And that was a very bad thing.

I pressed my palms to his chest and took a step back. As I nodded and tried to catch my breath, I answered, "Yeah. Wow, that guy was flying."

"You sure you're alright?" he confirmed.

"Hazards of living in a city like this," I remarked, trying to brush off the fact that I was still in shock that I'd nearly been hit by a car. "Thank you for reacting so quickly."

With a gentle dip of his chin, he asked, "Are you heading to the venue now?"

I gave him a nod in response and added, "I need to hurry because I've got to get to Priscilla before she starts losing her mind."

Realization dawned in his handsome face. He moved close to me and urged, "Let's get you in your car so you can get out of here then."

With that, I moved toward the driver side door of my car. I was acutely aware of the fact that Ben had moved his body behind mine so he was guarding me from the oncoming traffic. And if that gesture wasn't sweet enough, he put his hand on the small of my back and reached around me to open my door.

I quickly folded myself in.

"Be careful pulling out," he warned.

"I will. Thanks again."

Ben closed my door and stepped away. I pulled out when there was a break in the flow of traffic. But as I drove off, I glanced up in my rearview at the man who'd left me wondering if maybe I hadn't had the best first impression of him.

CHAPTER 2

Cora

I DIDN'T KNOW IF IT WAS BY SHEER LUCK OR THE FACT THAT I drove like a madwoman to the location of the reception to drop off the desserts, but I managed to avoid seeing Ben again. The reason for that could have also been that perhaps he didn't immediately go to the location to drop off the sweets he'd put in his car.

Whatever the reason, I counted my blessings and dashed over to meet Priscilla. And it was a blessing because Ben had thrown me completely off balance in the very short encounter we'd had. I hadn't expected him to be as kind and even chivalrous as he was.

I made it back to where Priscilla and the rest of her bridesmaids were getting themselves all done up. By the time I arrived, all of the girls had their hair done, one was still getting makeup done, and the rest were either getting dressed or helping Priscilla into her gown.

"I was so worried you weren't going to be back here on time," Priscilla shared when I entered the room.

Rolling my eyes at her, I asserted, "I told you I was going to be here with plenty of time to spare."

"Did you get the dress taken care of?" she asked.

Nodding, I replied, "Yep. I had just finished it when Sebastian called to tell me about the dessert truck."

Suddenly, it was like Priscilla remembered that I'd been out taking care of the desserts because her eyes widened curiously before she fretted, "Were you able to meet the driver and get everything squared away?"

I gave her a nod and smile.

From that point forward, Priscilla seemed to relax and enjoy the rest of the late morning with her friends and family members. I used the time to finish getting myself ready and to make sure all the loose ends were tied up.

When the florist delivered the bouquets, I confirmed that the arrangements had been delivered as scheduled to both the ceremony and reception locations. I confirmed the schedule for the day with the photographer and videographer before I reached out to the deejay one last time. After a few additional calls to individuals involved in making sure the day was going to run smoothly, it was time to get moving.

Priscilla had wanted to get the posed pictures done prior to the actual ceremony, so we all made our way down to the meeting location. The photographers were a husband and wife duo, so they organized a first-look session for Priscilla and Sebastian. Afterward, the rest of us had to follow instructions on where to stand and when to smile.

When we first arrived, I'd looked at Ben once. It was a mistake. He'd been eyeing me curiously. The second we made eye contact, his look went from curious to devious. He was flirting with me.

So, I quickly diverted my attention anywhere but him. I'd managed to do alright when it was simply just the bridesmaids with the bride, or the bridesmaids with the groom. Somehow, I succeeded in avoiding making eye contact with Ben. But soon enough, the girls had to pair up with the groomsmen.

That's when things took a turn.

Since I was paired up with Ben, there was more than one instance where I needed to stand right next to him. In every one of those cases, either my hands were touching him or, more often than not, his were on me. Thankfully, even though I'd heard my fair share of stories about the kind of guy Ben was, I found him to be extremely respectful in these moments.

And the more I was around him, the more I found myself reacting to his touch.

I was grateful that there was a constant buzz of conversation around us. If it weren't for that or the photographers instructing everyone where they needed to be, I had no doubt Ben would have engaged in more conversation than he did.

"I don't know about you, but I think this is all just a bit too much," he said quietly enough so that only I could hear him. Ben was standing behind me, one of his hands cupping my elbow. We were waiting for the photographers to get everyone else into position.

"The pictures?" I questioned him, my voice just a hair over a whisper.

"All of it," he answered.

I couldn't say I disagreed. But then again, I was surprised he felt that way. "I agree. It's a bit much for me personally, too."

Even though I wouldn't do this, I could still understand that there were a lot of people who would do all that Priscilla and Sebastian were doing. In fact, while they were one of my most ostentatious couples, I'd had a couple others that had them beat by miles. No matter what I thought, it was their wedding. If they wanted to celebrate something so important in their life by going over the top, it wasn't my place to talk them out of it. It would have been foolish to do so anyway. Because the bigger the wedding, the larger the budget. And that was always a good thing for me.

After we'd finished up with the pictures, the men and women went their separate ways. Everything had been timed perfectly because we had just enough time to get from where we'd taken pictures to where the ceremony was taking place.

When the piano started playing and the bridesmaids began walking down the aisle, I suddenly started feeling a bit anxious. It was hitting me then that, with the exception of Priscilla, Sebastian, their parents, and the bridesmaids, I didn't know anyone else. There were hundreds of people at this wedding.

Three hundred and twenty-nine to be exact.

Something came over me, and all I could do when it was my turn to walk down the aisle was look at someone familiar.

That someone was Ben Mason.

I didn't want to. I tried not to.

But there were so many people.

And he was the only familiar face I could find that I didn't think would make me look like an awkward fool. Of course, to him I probably seemed like one, but I figured one person thinking that was better than hundreds. Even if that person was Ben.

If Ben thought anything negative about me keeping my eyes glued to him, he didn't let it show. There was something in his face that resembled intrigue. I knew that was probably dangerous. I just couldn't bring myself to look away from him.

I made it to the end of the aisle and took my place next to the other bridesmaids. While we waited for the final bridesmaid and the maid-of-honor to walk down the aisle, my eyes slid to the man standing across the aisle from me. I hadn't expected that he'd be staring right back at me.

I did all I could do to tear my gaze from his and back down to the end of the aisle.

Once Priscilla made her way to her groom, I managed to pull myself together. I stayed that way through the remainder of the ceremony.

Of course, I was right back to square one after the newlyweds shared their first kiss as husband and wife and turned to leave. The bridal party began filing out behind them. I kept moving closer to the aisle as the girls in front of me met their groomsman and took off.

Then, I locked eyes with Ben. He gave me a smile

and held out his arm to me. I slid my hand through and linked my arm with his. I liked the way it felt, and I loved the way he smelled.

A lot.

And that was so very bad.

I needed to get away from him.

Fast.

As soon as we were outside and away from the crowd, I walked up to Priscilla and Sebastian. After offering congratulatory words to them, I explained, "I'm going to head over and make sure everything is squared away for the reception before everybody makes their way over there."

"It's okay, Cora," Priscilla declared. "I'm sure everything is fine. I thought all that stuff was important, but I'm married now. That's all that matters."

In any other scenario, I'd have been ecstatic to hear those words. Not today. Not when I needed to get away from the man who smelled delightful.

I shook my head and insisted, "No. It's my job. I'm going to go over just to be sure. I'll see you in a few minutes."

"Fine," she agreed. "But promise me you're going to try and enjoy yourself after that."

"Of course," I lied. "Once I'm confident that everything is running smoothly, I'll enjoy myself."

With that, and without another look back, I took off. As I had expected, there wasn't anything that needed my attention. Between the professionalism of the venue and the fact that I'd been on top of them about the wedding for quite some time now, I didn't actually expect that there would have been any problems. In fact, I'd worked with them before for another wedding, so I hadn't really had any doubts about their ability to make sure everything went off without a hitch. However, since I needed the distraction, I pretended that there was a reason to follow through with them.

I found a way to keep myself occupied with small tasks up until it was time for the bridal party to be announced. Following our introductions, Priscilla and Sebastian were going to have their first dance together. Then, the rest of the bridal party would join in for a dance.

When I had to slip my hand through Ben's arm a second time, I silently cursed at myself for my willingness to go against my rules and for allowing Priscilla to talk me into becoming an official bridesmaid. Of course, if I hadn't agreed, then someone else would have been standing here with Ben.

My eyes widened at the thought. I had no idea why that would have even bothered me, but it did.

With all the commotion around us, there was no way Ben and I could have had a conversation. I was only partially relieved because every time I was around him, I was noticing something else new that I was drawn to. And considering we couldn't really talk as we were waiting for our introduction, I found myself taking in Ben's physical appearance.

I had to give him credit. He was stunning, so perhaps not everything I'd heard about him was a lie.

Ben was tall, dark, and handsome. His cobalt blue eyes had mesmerized me from the first moment he looked at me. Those eyes combined with his pronounced jawline, thick black hair, and his tall, lean, muscular build made me wonder if he hadn't stepped off the set of a soap opera. It was hard to believe men who looked like Ben actually existed in the world. Nevertheless, being able to gaze at him was no hardship, so I decided to look on the bright side.

After Priscilla and Sebastian danced their first dance together, the deejay asked the bridal party to join the newlyweds on the dance floor.

No sooner had Ben slipped an arm around my waist and pulled me close when he shared, "I'm not a big dancer, but the second I realized you were the one who filled in for Priscilla's cousin, I couldn't wait to get to this part of the night."

My lips parted in shock. "Really?"

Ben offered a dip of his chin in response. "So, how do you know her?" he asked.

"Who?" I stupidly asked.

Letting out a little laugh, Ben clarified, "The bride."

"She hired me."

He jerked his head back. "Pardon?"

Grinning because I knew his head was about to explode, I clarified, "I met her about a year ago when she hired me for the wedding."

"She hired you to be in her wedding?" he asked, completely confused.

I shook my head. "No. I have a very strict policy about that."

He cocked a questioning eyebrow at me. "I don't understand then."

"I'm a professional bridesmaid," I told him.

"A professional bridesmaid?" he repeated.

Nodding, I answered, "Yeah. Basically, brides hire me to handle all the things bridesmaids typically would. So, I take care of everything from dealing with the other professionals, such as the photographer, caterer, baker, and deejay, to helping with the guest list, planning the bridal shower and bachelorette party, and even helping the bride use the bathroom on her big day."

"Wow. That sounds like a nightmare."

I shrugged. "It's not that bad. I actually enjoy most of it. Besides, I've learned a lot and now know what I will and won't do if I ever get married."

Ben let out a laugh. "So, if you have a strict policy about not being in the wedding, how did you end up here in my arms?"

Well, if that wasn't a loaded question...

"As you know, Priscilla's cousin, Cecilia, ended up in the hospital needing emergency surgery," I began. "And with it being such a last-minute ordeal, the bride ended up in my office yesterday begging me. She refused to take no for an answer, and since I couldn't locate another professional to fill in on such short notice, I had no choice."

"Well, I'm glad you felt you couldn't tell her to take a hike," he remarked through an amused chuckle.

"I couldn't," I assured him. When he returned a dubious look, I challenged, "Have you ever been around

Priscilla when she's worked up and ranting about something?"

Ben's face instantly changed. Suddenly, he looked like he felt sorry for me. "Point made."

It was then that I felt a tap on my arm as Priscilla declared, "I knew you two would get along great. The song ended like thirty seconds ago and you two haven't separated."

I instantly stepped out of Ben's arms and looked up at him, mortified.

Priscilla didn't seem to notice or care because she went on, "I need to use the ladies' room before we sit down for dinner. Can you help me, Cora?"

I gave her a nod, looked back to Ben, and stated sarcastically, "Work perks."

He laughed again. "I'll catch you later."

I smiled at him and replied, "Thanks for the dance and the conversation."

With that, I left Ben there so I could help the bride with her dress. When we returned, dinner was being served. We both sat down to eat. Following dinner, the real festivities began. I didn't get too involved. I mostly stood back and watched. It's not that I didn't enjoy dancing; I simply didn't really know anyone well enough.

When a couple of slow songs were played, Ben asked me to dance with him. Since he was being nice, and I enjoyed talking with him, I figured there was no harm in it.

But as the evening wound down, I should have suspected things would change. Once a lot of the guests had left for the night and the bride and groom were preparing to head to their newlywed suite, Ben approached me.

"I really thought this was going to be a nightmare tonight," he shared.

"It wasn't so bad," I returned.

He took a few steps toward me, ran his knuckles along the bare skin of my arm, and agreed, "No, it wasn't."

I swallowed hard at the intimate touch from him.

Ben continued, "I had a fantastic time with you tonight, Cora. And I'd really love to see you again."

No.

No. No. No.

"I had a nice time, too. But I don't think it's a good idea for us to get together again beyond tonight," I stated.

His expression went from hopeful and excited to disappointed and a bit shocked.

"Is there something wrong?" he wondered.

Shaking my head, I assured him, "No, not at all. It's just, I'm not really looking to get involved in anything serious right now."

"Well, that's not normally my thing either. But I didn't think you were the kind of woman who'd agree to coming home with me only hours after meeting me," he reasoned. "I figured there'd be no harm in getting together again outside of the wedding so we could get to know each other better."

Wow. I really hadn't expected that from him.

Before I could respond, he went on, "If all you're

looking for is something casual, I can accommodate that, too."

He ended with a sly grin.

"Nice try," I praised him. "But I think this is where things are going to end between us."

Ben eyed me for a few long seconds before he muttered under his breath, "Damn, this is hard."

I didn't know what that meant, but I wasn't sure it was wise of me to ask either. So, wanting to touch him one last time, I pressed my hand to his chest, gave him a sweet smile, and repeated, "I had a great time, Ben. Have a good night."

At that, I turned and walked away. And I didn't look back. Because I knew if I did, I would have changed my mind.

Ben

This hadn't ever happened to me.

For the first time in my adult life, a woman was walking away from me. Over the years, I'd grown accustomed to the fact that I could simply give a woman a smile and a wink, and I'd have her willing to go anywhere to do anything. I'd done that many times.

And it worked for a long time.

I got what I wanted, and the women usually got more than they imagined.

But something had changed recently. Finally, after years of meaningless hook ups, I was beginning to crave something more. I wasn't sure where the desire to settle down was coming from; I just knew that I wanted to find someone with whom I could share my life.

And to do that, I was going to need to find someone unlike most of the other women I'd been with. Someone who was interested in me for something other than just my money or a night of fun.

Because that's how it had been. People may have looked at me as a player, and to some extent, I guess they were right. But I'd been used just as much by the women who were with me. I knew it, but I didn't care.

Now at the age of thirty-five though, I wanted a woman who could go the distance.

I had a feeling that Cora could be that woman.

She was obviously beautiful, but it was her cautious nature and the almost cynical outlook she had that really drew me in. It wasn't in a bad way, however. I knew the instant we were taking pictures with the bridal party that she was doing what she had to do, but she was not truly enjoying herself. So, when I expressed my feelings on it, I wasn't exactly surprised to hear her agreeing with me.

Once I had more time to talk with her as the night went on, my need to get to know her better only grew. I didn't know if she knew anything about me, so I wanted to tread cautiously.

But I never imagined I wouldn't have the opportunity to try.

Because she shot me down.

And that was something I'd never experienced.

Of course, I was Ben Mason. I didn't become this successful because I gave up when things got tough.

Nope.

I always got what I wanted.

And what I wanted now was a shot at something meaningful with Cora Daniels.

CHAPTER 3

Cora

I T WAS LATE TUESDAY MORNING, AND I WAS SITTING IN ONE of the cafés just two blocks away from my office. Whenever I needed a change of scenery, I'd venture out and try to get some work done wherever I thought I'd find some creative inspiration.

Luckily, working in Manhattan meant that there was no shortage of inspiration everywhere I looked. It was one of the things I loved most about being in the city. Of course, I had plans to eventually move outside the city, but right now I was focused on building my business and earning a living. If the time came that I met the right person and I had the opportunity to plan my own wedding, I'd certainly want to make moves to live on the outskirts of the hustle and bustle knowing I'd be able to drop in anytime I wanted. No matter what type of atmosphere I was seeking, there was always a place I could go to find it.

Sometimes, I'd head over to Central Park if I was craving fresh air. But today, I needed caffeine because I hadn't been sleeping much.

Ever since Priscilla's wedding three days ago, I'd been finding it difficult to get a restful night of sleep. I knew why, but I hated to admit it, even to myself.

Ben Mason.

I hadn't been able to get him out of my mind. I knew it had everything to do with regret.

Regret that I'd turned him down at the end of the night. That I hadn't even been willing to give myself the opportunity for another chance to find happiness. I wanted it; I truly hoped to one day find it.

But Ben was a risk. A big one I wasn't sure I could survive if I took a chance and things went south between us. Especially if they ended the way my last relationship did.

And with Ben's reputation, it was a very strong possibility that I'd be letting history repeat itself.

As I sat next to the picture window at the front of the café fueling my body with its source of energy for the next few hours, I worked. I had a couple of weddings over the next several months, but it wasn't anything overwhelming. Part of that was because none of my upcoming brides were anything like Priscilla, in both personality and wealth. The other part was that Priscilla's mid-October wedding was the last big one of the season. While there were a few over the next several months, wedding season had almost officially ended for me with the one where I'd met the man I couldn't get out of my head.

I'd been working for a good hour when I heard, "Cora?"

The sound of a voice I'd grown to love and then

ultimately hate filled me with dread. I looked up, saw him, and my body instantly tensed.

Joshua Collins.

Otherwise known as my slimeball ex-boyfriend.

Of course, that was purely my biased opinion, but that didn't make it any less accurate. While others might have disagreed with me, I knew the truth of just who he was.

To everyone else, Josh was a handsome, rich, and successful businessman. He'd made a fortune off his restaurant business. As the owner of two of the city's most highly-patronized restaurants and another slated to open before the end of the year, Josh had proven himself to be a master at his craft.

Being good-looking and, though it pains me to admit it, great in bed, Josh was quite the catch. And I'd managed to land him.

Or so I thought.

As it turned out, he had me for three years, but I never had him.

I had fallen in love and given him the best of me, and in the end, he turned out to be a cheater. Not just with one woman either. He'd had multiple women, and I was just one of them. Not anyone special or worthy of more than just the piece of jewelry he could buy me. Sure, it was nice, but I would have given that up if it meant I'd have his love in return.

I thought I had it. He knew how to play the part of the loving and devoted boyfriend so well. Not only did he give me lavish gifts, but he'd made time for me when

I needed it. In my profession, though, my weekends during wedding season were typically busy. That meant assuming the role of doting lover was easy for Josh because my free time wasn't difficult to accommodate. And when the weekends rolled around, he was free to find a new woman to make his latest, greatest dish.

So, while each piece of jewelry he'd given me over the years might have seemed like a nice, loving gesture, it was always simply a way for him to make himself feel better about what he was doing to me.

Looking up at him now, I felt nothing but disgust.

I'd left him nearly a year ago, and I was not the least bit sorry about it.

The only problem at the moment was that he was standing there, still looking great, and he had a woman with him. One who didn't even seem to realize she was in a public place. With the way she was all over him, it was like they'd just rolled out of bed. Considering he never went to his restaurants until just before the lunch rush hit, it wouldn't have been a wrong assumption to believe that's precisely what had happened either.

"Yes?" I asked.

Like he didn't even have a woman standing beside him, he marveled, "Wow, it's been a long time. You look great."

I blinked in surprise.

Was he joking?

"I'm sorry?"

"How have you been?" he questioned me.

"Josh?" the woman breathed in his ear. When he

glanced in her direction, she declared, "I'm going to run to the ladies' room while you catch up with your friend."

I cocked an eyebrow and mumbled, "He's *not* my friend."

She didn't hear me.

I watched as she walked away but looked back up to find Josh's gaze following her. From the look on his face, he was clearly recalling whatever happened between them either last night or early this morning. When he returned his gaze to me, he said, "I heard about the Galloway wedding. Everyone has been raving about it. I'm sure that was all you."

I didn't know if he was expecting a response, but I didn't give him one. It's not like he'd asked a question.

When he realized I wasn't making a move to respond, he pulled out the chair opposite of me and sat down. "You can't possibly still be mad at me, Cora," he noted. "It's been a year. I apologized. You need to at least be cordial."

"I don't *need* to do anything for you, Josh," I bit out. "The time for me doing anything for you has long since passed."

"Well, you're obviously not over me or you wouldn't be this bitter still," he reasoned.

"Oh, I'm over you," I insisted.

He clasped his hands together on the table and leaned in. Evidently, he didn't believe I was being honest because his voice got low and he offered, "Cora, if you haven't moved on and you miss what we had, I'm willing to make some time for you."

My eyes widened in disbelief. I began wondering if he was always this stupid and perhaps I was just too blinded by love to see it.

Before I could say anything, he added, "Maybe we don't work as a couple, but—"

I cut him off and spat, "We didn't work as a couple because you couldn't keep it in your pants, asshole."

Completely unbothered by that, Josh remarked, "You were one of the best I've had. If you change your mind, you know how to find me."

One of the best he had. Boy, did that make me feel special.

"Don't hold your breath," I shot back.

Just then, I felt a hand on my shoulder as a familiar voice I'd craved for the last three days interrupted the conversation. "Cora, baby, so sorry I'm late. I got tied up at work."

I looked up and had barely a moment to register what was happening before Ben pressed a sweet kiss to my lips. When he pulled back, he gave me a wink and smiled at me.

That wink.

My goodness, that wink.

I couldn't begin to process anything that was going on, but I liked that he had taken charge.

Ben took his attention from me to Josh and held out his hand. "Hi, I'm—"

"Benjamin Mason," Josh cut him off, not reaching out to shake Ben's hand. At that point, the woman who'd arrived with Josh had returned from the restroom. I saw her eyeing up Ben, but he wasn't paying her any attention. Even still, I felt oddly possessive and wished I had the ability to shoot daggers from my eyes at her.

"And you are?" Ben asked Josh.

Josh stood, came to just about eyelevel with Ben and stated proudly, "Josh Collins."

The woman with Josh added, "He owns The Grillehouse and Collins Bistro, and he's got another restaurant opening at the beginning of December."

Ben's brows shot up curiously. "Really? What kind of cuisine? Maybe Cora and I can check them out sometime."

I was surprised that Ben hadn't heard of either of the restaurants. It wasn't very often that someone hadn't been familiar with them. As a New Yorker, even if he had no idea who Josh was, it was unexpected that Ben hadn't heard of the restaurants.

Josh's eyes diverted to mine. "Cora knows. She's been to both before and can fill you in."

"Great," Ben returned happily.

A moment of silence passed as Josh, with his disbelieving gaze, allowed himself to really study my face. I'm not sure what he saw, but I was hoping he realized what he lost and would never have again.

"Wait a minute," Ben broke the silence. When he had everyone's attention, he shared, "I do recognize your name, Josh. It just came to me. You're on the list of attendees for the Fleming Foundation charity benefit this Thursday."

Josh grew confident again. He was always so proud

whenever anyone recognized him. "That's right," he confirmed. "I try to make sure I give back to important causes. I'm donating half a million. I'm surprised to see you weren't on the list."

Ben returned, "Well, I guess I can leak the news. As a huge supporter of the foundation, I had every intention of going. When I was approached about attending, the organizers wanted to keep it a secret. I pledged my donation amount, and they want to make a big thing about it. So, I'll be there, but it's supposed to be a surprise. Cora and I have been looking forward to this event for a while now. I guess we'll see you there."

I couldn't believe it. Ben was using this situation with Josh to get me to go on a date with him.

"Josh?" the woman with him called. "I need some coffee."

Ben didn't hesitate to respond. "Please don't let us keep you. It was nice meeting you, Josh. We'll see you around."

"Likewise," Josh returned without any of the same sincerity.

He gave me one last glance before he slid his arm around the waist of his woman and moved away from my table.

Like it was no big deal, Ben parked himself in the seat across from me.

"What did you just do?" I asked.

He was grinning from ear to ear. "I saved you for a second time," he replied.

"Saved me?"

Ben nodded and added, "Yeah. The first time I saved your life when someone tried to run you over. This time was much better, though. Because lucky for me, this time you weren't in physical danger, and I got a kiss out of it."

"Yeah, let's talk about that for a minute," I began. "Why did you do that?"

I didn't get an answer. Ben just stared at me, assessing me. When too much time had passed without a reply, I questioned, "Why are you looking at me like that?"

"I'm trying to figure out if you're serious," he returned.

"I am."

Throwing his hand out to the side to point in the direction Josh had gone, Ben explained, "I walked in, heard the way that guy was talking to you, knew you weren't comfortable and decided to step in. After listening to the things he was saying, I thought it was best to put him in his place."

"And kissing me factored into that how?" I wondered.

Ben's shoulders fell. "Was it not a good kiss?" he retorted.

It was. It was magnificent.

"That's not the point," I debated.

"It's exactly the point," he challenged with a grin on his face. "You know just as well as I do what that kiss felt like. If that's the first one, and it felt that good to us, imagine what it looked like to him."

I hadn't considered that.

"Okay. So, you thought you'd catch me off guard so you could kiss me?"

Ben shook his head, a wave of disappointment flooding his features. "No, Cora. I kissed you because from what I could tell, you had a relationship with that guy. Based on what I heard, he was an asshole in the biggest way possible, ending whatever you had between the two of you. He was standing here trying to humiliate you, acting like he is something special. I know who Josh Collins is, baby. A man like him is not one who likes having a blow to his ego."

He knew Josh?

"You acted like you had no idea who he was," I pointed out.

"Exactly. But you do realize he knew just who I was, right? He was already feeling insignificant when I stepped up and kissed you. For whatever reason, that guy thinks he's better than you. He genuinely believes you are lucky to be in his presence. So, I just made sure he felt less important than he already is. The fact that you moved on to me is not sitting well with him right now."

Ben glanced to the side and saw Josh standing there looking back at us. He slid his seat closer to mine. His back was to Josh when he brought a hand up to cup my cheek. He gently stroked his thumb along my cheek.

I tried to ignore that and reminded him, "But I didn't move on to you."

Ben grinned and continued to caress my skin. "He doesn't know that."

My lips parted as I realized that Ben decided to stand in as my fake boyfriend just to help me make a grand statement to my ex.

Ben leaned in closer. I whispered, "What are you doing?"

"Showing him that he was the lucky one."

"Ben…" I trailed off.

"Kiss me, Cora. Kiss me and show him what he gets to regret for the rest of his life," Ben urged.

Between his words and the gentle strokes of his thumb over my cheek, I couldn't stop myself.

I closed the distance between us and touched my mouth to his. Apparently, I had no shame either because the minute I felt his tongue, my lips parted and allowed him access. Perhaps I was a bit like the woman Josh had walked in with. Because while Ben kissed me, nothing else existed. It didn't seem to matter that I was sitting at the front window in a coffee shop on a busy New York City street. All that mattered was how much Ben excelled at kissing.

When he tore his mouth from mine, he declared, "If you plan to keep up this charade, you're going to have to play the part and get a dress for Thursday evening."

I swallowed hard, my lips just barely grazing his. "Okay," I rasped.

"And for the record," he started. "Seeing how he treated you today, I've got to tell you, I hope you plan to do just that because I do not like that guy."

Instead of answering with words, I smiled against his lips before I kissed him again to show my agreement.

CHAPTER 4

Cora

"WHAT DO YOU THINK, KENZ?" I ASKED.

"About the dress or the guy?" my best friend, Mackenzie, returned.

Looking in the fitting room mirror at the dress I currently had on, I already knew I wasn't going to get the dress. "About Ben," I clarified.

I moved toward Kenzie so she could help me unzip the dress. As she pulled the zipper down the side, she answered, "I think you should go to this charity benefit tomorrow and enjoy yourself."

"Right, I already planned on that. But what if Ben ends up doing to me what Josh did?" I questioned her. "I can't go through that again."

While I slipped off and stepped out of the dress, she asked, "Are you saying that you're never going to give yourself the chance to fall in love again because one guy was an asshole?"

"Of course not," I assured her. "It's just that Ben and Josh are a lot alike. Ben isn't exactly what I'd consider a safe choice."

I had just pulled another dress up my body and settled the straps over my shoulders. After Kenzie zipped it up the back, she debated, "From everything you just told me about what happened yesterday morning, I don't think Ben and Josh are alike at all. Aside from the fact that they both have money and Ben's wealth, presumably, being considerably more, there isn't much else you said that would make me believe that they are similar. But does any of that really matter right now? You're merely going with him to one function. I don't think you're at the point where you need to be worried about this. If you find that things start to get serious, just talk to him about it before it goes too far."

I didn't necessarily believe that Ben and Josh were replicas of each other, but it was no secret that Ben had been with a lot of women. When I shared this concern with Kenzie, she defended him. "Listen, I obviously only know what one can hear living in this city. I don't know Ben personally, but the minute you told me what happened yesterday morning, I did my job as your best friend and scoured the internet for anything I could find on him. Based on what I've seen, there is no denying he's had a lot of women. He's been involved in a lot of functions like the one you'll be heading to tomorrow, but not once did I see him in a photo with the same woman twice. That tells me that he's either not found someone he wants to be serious with, or he's not interested in being serious with someone."

That's what concerned me. I hadn't been able to bring myself to search him on the internet. I knew

Kenzie would do that for me and share anything that she found concerning. Hearing he'd been photographed with a lot of women did not make me feel good things.

"That's not making me feel all warm and fuzzy, Kenz," I told her.

"So what? You can't deny yourself the opportunity to go on a date with a man because he has a past, Cora. If it worries you, talk to him about it. He obviously already knows what you've been through with Josh, so I don't think he'd take offense to you asking for clarification on his intentions. As your best friend, it's my job to tell you if I think you're making a mistake. I don't think that's what this is at all. I mean, he stepped in to play the part of your boyfriend when he saw your ex trying to humiliate you. That's got to count for something."

It did.

It really did.

But I didn't want to find myself caught up in a mess of uncertainty about where things were with Ben and me. I wasn't confused about his interest in me because he'd made that perfectly clear. My concerns were about whether he was only showing interest to make me another notch on his bedpost.

From the moment I'd met him, he'd been incredibly sweet. Not only did he provide good conversation and company at the wedding, but he also came to my rescue in two separate incidences. So, like Kenzie said, it all counted for something.

That was precisely my dilemma. Because I knew with the way he kissed that I was too curious about what else he was good at not to want to take things another step further with him. But if it was just going to be a one-night stand for him, that was not something I was interested in. Mostly because I didn't think my heart could handle it. Especially not with the way I'd been thinking about him for the last few days.

"This dress is not the one either," I stated.

"Agreed. Let me run out and grab you one other that I saw. It's a little daring, but I totally think you could pull it off. And if it fits the way I think it will, you'll have that man falling at your feet."

Shaking my head in disbelief, I reminded her, "He's made it known he likes me, Kenz. I don't think I need a dress to try to entice him."

She shrugged. "It won't hurt. Besides, if you tell him where you are, emotionally speaking, and he's not there, maybe the promise of you in dresses, like the one I'm about to bring in here, moving forward might have him changing his mind."

"I think I'd rather have him wanting to be on the same page as me for reasons that have nothing to do with what I'm wearing, though."

Kenzie took a few steps toward me. She took my hand in hers and said softly, "I know, Cora. But you've got to give him the opportunity to get to know you. I'm not telling you to jump in the bed with the guy on the first date if that's not something you are prepared to do. But don't miss the chance to show him just how amazing you are. Because Ben didn't get to where he is in his life by being stupid. And a smart man wouldn't let you pass him by."

My head tilted to the side, and I smiled before I rasped, "Love you, Kenzie."

Grinning at me, she replied, "Keep that in mind when I bring in this dress."

With that, she spun on her heels and dashed out of the dressing room. I stood there and thought about my conversation with her while I waited for her to return. And when I put on the gown she'd brought in five minutes later, I had no doubts that she was the best friend I'd ever have.

I slipped my feet into the strappy four-inch heels I'd decided to wear with the gown I purchased yesterday. Just as I finished securing the strap on the second sandal, I heard a sound fill the apartment.

Ben was here.

I buzzed him up and moved to my full-length mirror to take one last look at myself. There was no denying that the dress Kenzie had found was a perfect fit. It was a long, red, satin dress. There was a two-inch wide section of fabric that covered the top of my shoulder. From there, the material came down over my breasts forming a deep-V plunging neckline. It had an empire waist, so while it was more form-fitting up top, the bottom cascaded down loosely to the floor. Standing there, it looked pretty simple. But when I walked, that's where the magic happened. There were two slits in the dress that came to the upper part of my thigh. As I took each step, my leg became exposed.

I looked great.

I just hoped that Ben didn't think the dress was too over-the-top.

When I heard the knock at the door, I took in a deep breath before I moved to it.

"Hey," I greeted Ben after I opened the door and stepped back to allow him to come inside. "You have perfect timing."

He came in far enough that I was able to close the door behind him, but he didn't make any move beyond that. Ben simply stood there, staring at me. I allowed him to do it mostly because I was taking him in at the same time.

The man was pure perfection. Top to toe, there wasn't anything about him that didn't work for me.

"You look beautiful, Cora," he finally declared, his voice a mix of a deep, sexy rumble and something else I couldn't quite figure out.

"Thank you, Ben. You look fantastic as well."

His eyes roamed over my face a few seconds before he asked, "You ready to go?"

Returning a nod, I replied, "Yes. Let me just grab my bag, and we can leave."

I turned to move back through my apartment so I could get my clutch. As I started walking away, I heard Ben mutter, "Fuck."

I stopped and turned back around. "Excuse me?"

Ben shook his head and said, "Nothing."

I eyed him a moment, wondering if he was going to give in and tell me what he was swearing about, but he didn't. So, I sought out my purse and returned to where Ben was still standing just inside the door. Once there, he opened the door and put his hand to the small of my back. His hand touched my naked skin there because the dress had an open back. That touch sent shivers through me.

A few minutes later, Ben and I were sitting in his fancy two-seater on the way to the charity event.

"What kind of car is this?" I asked.

"A McLaren Senna."

"Sounds as expensive as it looks," I remarked.

Ben let out a laugh. "It is."

"I had a feeling that was the case," I began. "But can you explain something to me?"

We were stopped in traffic, so Ben glanced over and said, "I can try."

"How is it that you thought Priscilla and Sebastian's wedding was too much, but this is not?"

Grinning at me, he explained, "First of all, that wedding was entirely too much. You even agreed with me. This car is not too much. A wedding is one day, but I'll have this car for much longer than that."

A car behind us honked so Ben started driving again. That's when I argued, "But a wedding is a very important day in someone's life. Yes, I agreed that Priscilla's was a bit over-the-top, but that doesn't mean I believe a wedding is just another day either. And, let's be honest, a wedding is the start of something that is meant to be a life-long commitment. So, presumably, the marriage should outlast the car."

"I'm not saying that a wedding is just like any other day," he assured me. "But it is *a* day. It's about the two people who are committing themselves to each other. It shouldn't be about overdoing it simply so they can impress everyone else."

I couldn't say he didn't have a point. I'd thought about the day I'd finally get married for a long time. There was a point in my life when I thought Josh was going to be the man I'd marry. Obviously, that didn't happen, but when I look back now, I realize that if it had gotten to that point, he would have wanted it to be something extravagant just because it could be.

"Well, you should have explained it like that in the first place," I noted.

Fifteen minutes later, we'd arrived at the event. Ben ushered me inside, his hand at the small of my back again. I did my best to try and ignore what his touch did to me because I didn't want to fall on my face. I didn't need to work too hard at it because no sooner did we step inside when I lost his hand.

Ben was a very popular man. The minute he was spotted, he had a constant flow of individuals coming up to him. I didn't officially know anyone he'd conversed with, but I recognized some of them simply because of who they were. And no matter that he had to do it so many times, Ben introduced me to every single person who'd come up to talk with him.

We managed to get a break long enough to be able

to grab drinks. But we'd both barely taken a sip before Ben was pulled into another conversation.

Eventually, though, everyone was ushered into the main dining hall. That was when I saw Josh. Surprisingly, he was with the same woman he'd been with at the café. When Josh saw me, something came over his face. Whatever it was, lasted only a few seconds before it was gone and replaced by something else. When I felt Ben's hand slide around my back and land on my opposite hip, I realized what the look on Josh's face was.

Bitterness.

And perhaps a touch of jealousy.

My eyes left Josh, and I tipped my head back to look up at Ben. He was looking down at me smiling. Knowing how clever and observant he was, I assumed he was trying to put a show on for Josh. Following his lead, I beamed up at him and even leaned my body into his side. Ben took my weight and gave my hip a gentle squeeze.

"Let's go grab our seats," he urged before leading us through the mass of tables to one that was reserved near the front of the room.

Ben and I were seated with the organizers of the event and founders of the foundation, Gavin and Amara Fleming. I'd been introduced to the both of them along with a few other members, but dinner was served almost immediately after we'd sat down. They wanted to be sure they stayed on schedule, so there wasn't much opportunity for conversation beyond them being extremely welcoming and thankful. Even still, I managed to learn a little bit about the foundation.

"Thank you so much for attending tonight, Cora," Amara said.

I smiled and gave her a nod. "Absolutely. I'm honored to be here, but I have to admit I just learned about the existence of the foundation and don't know much about it."

Amara didn't seem to take any offense and shared, "Five years ago, my life changed forever. My nineteen-year-old daughter, Heidi, died of a drug overdose."

I gasped. "Oh, I'm so sorry to hear that."

"Thank you," she returned. "Gavin and I had been trying for years to get her the help she needed. The first time, we got her into rehab, and she stayed clean for seven months before relapsing. We did it again. She stayed clean three months. And again. The last time she was clean for a full fourteen months. We thought we'd finally made the breakthrough, but the first time she used again after that, she overdosed. My husband and I couldn't sit back and do nothing. We needed to find a way to honor her, so we created the foundation. Rehabilitation is a long process that requires the best care possible. There are a lot of individuals, like Heidi, who would benefit from a longer, more intensive rehab. Unfortunately, it comes at a cost. We wanted to find a way to help those people who want to get clean. Heidi wanted it. She tried really hard. But in the end, her addiction got the best of her."

My heart broke for Amara. I hadn't ever had any experiences with drug addiction. Nobody in my family had either, so I never put a lot of thought into it. Hearing

Heidi's story opened my eyes to the reality of it and just how much of an ongoing process and struggle it must be.

"I can't imagine the pain and heartache you've gone through. I can't imagine that it's easy for you, but I imagine it brings you comfort to know you're doing something to help others in a similar situation. I find it admirable," I replied.

Amara confirmed, "It's certainly trying. I have days that I struggle personally to even want to get out of bed. I give myself that time to grieve, but somehow I find a way not to sit in it for too long."

Before I could respond, Gavin interrupted, "Amara, sweetheart, it's time to get the presentation started."

She gave him a nod and turned back to me. "It was lovely chatting with you, Cora."

"You too," I returned.

With that, Amara and Gavin stood, put their hands in one another's, and excused themselves before they moved to the podium at the front of the room.

"Good evening, everyone," Gavin began. "Thank you so much for your attendance here tonight. My wife and I along with the members of the board are truly overwhelmed and grateful for the support you've all shown for our cause. Illicit drug use, especially among our youth, is a huge epidemic in the city, and we wouldn't be able to do what we're doing if it weren't for all of you. Give yourselves a hand."

The room erupted in a round of applause.

When it died down, he continued, "As you all know,

your donations will go a long way in helping to ensure that these kids are able to go to top-notch rehabilitation centers, where they'll receive the best possible care and have the greatest chance of success."

Gavin continued talking about the goals and mission of the charity. I listened intently and was surprised when he said, "And now, I'd like to turn the mic over to our guest of honor, Benjamin Mason. As our largest supporter with his one-million-dollar donation, we wanted to give him the opportunity to speak on behalf of a cause that's evidently very important to him."

My eyes shot to Ben's. He gave me a wink and a smile before he stood and walked to the podium as everyone clapped for him.

Once he was standing before everyone, silence filled the room.

"Thank you," he began. "When Gavin and Amara approached me a little while ago about this event, I didn't hesitate to tell them that I wanted to be part of it. I've been contributing to the Fleming Foundation ever since the day I learned about it. Twenty-two years ago, I was only thirteen years old. I had a cousin I looked up to that was just three years older than me. Jasper and I were inseparable from the moment I could walk and talk. But five months after his sixteenth birthday, he got involved with the wrong people. All the things you hear about that happen when someone starts using happened with him. At the time, I had no idea what was going on. I just knew that he started spending less and less time with me and more time with his new friends. I hesitate to call them that because they weren't. Sadly, before I even turned sixteen, Jasper died of a drug overdose."

Oh my God.

My heart broke for Ben.

"My family and Jasper's family worked tirelessly to try and help him. He had gotten to that point where he wanted the help; he wanted to get clean. Unfortunately, times were tough years ago, and our families didn't have the money to send Jasper to the best places that would be able to help rehabilitate him with high levels of success. Jasper tried. He really did. But without the proper support system beyond his loving and devoted family, it didn't matter. I don't want access to a highly-qualified facility to ever be denied to someone who has the desire to get clean. It is my hope that with all of the money raised at this event, we'll be able to provide assistance to families who need it, so nobody ever has to go through what my family did."

Ben paused a moment before he ended, "Thank you."

The room filled with the sound of applause as Ben made his way back over to me. As Ben walked back, Amara had thanked him for sharing his story. Ben gave a wave and a nod before he leaned down and whispered in my ear, "Come with me."

Instantly, I stood. Ben linked his fingers with mine and led me out of the dining hall. I remained quiet as he headed down the hall to a set of glass double doors. He pushed through and stepped out onto the balcony. Once there, Ben moved to the stone wall at the edge and looked out into the garden landscape.

He still hadn't let go of my hand.

When too much time had passed without a word from him, I called, "Ben?"

His head turned in my direction.

"I'm sorry to hear about Jasper," I offered my condolences.

"Thanks. It was a long time ago, but it's never easy to talk about it."

I gave him a nod of understanding but didn't say anything else. I figured Ben needed whatever it was he was getting from standing out here on the balcony away from the crowd. Given the fact that he'd saved my life not quite a week ago and then stepped in to play the part of my boyfriend when Josh was being a jerk, I decided to give Ben my silent support. It was the least I could do.

Unfortunately, in doing it, I had time to think about the man standing beside me. And what I realized for the second time was that Ben wasn't anything like I had presumed him to be.

CHAPTER 5

Cora

LIVING IN A PLACE LIKE MANHATTAN, I ALWAYS FOUND myself drawn to the immense variety of people. It was one of the things I loved most about living in the city. With so many people packed into just over twenty-two square miles, it was impossible to walk even one block without being able to see the rich culture.

And in all of that, the one thing that always called to me was the fashion.

Considering the cost of living in New York City was already high, I had to get creative when it came to fashion. I refused to spend hundreds of dollars on one item, whether it be a jacket, shoes, or handbag. But the temptation was strong because I genuinely loved so many of the styles and trends that graced the streets of my beloved city.

So, I always found a way to tailor my looks to match some of my favorites at a bargain. But there were rare occasions where I might find myself splurging. In most of those cases, it is usually because I've seen a timeless piece that withstands the changing seasons and will become a staple in my wardrobe. The other cases where I've splurged were for the special occasions, such as the one two nights ago with Ben.

Today, however, was going to be a day where I paired some of my favorite fall trends with a classic New York City date. Because Ben was taking me to a Broadway musical.

I'd finally given in.

Following Ben's speech and subsequent moments of silence on the balcony at the charity event on Thursday, he asked me if I'd reconsider and give us a chance to get to know one another better.

"How can I convince you to change your mind?" he asked.

Dropping my head to the side, my curiosity getting the best of me, I returned, "About what?"

"Going on a date with me."

I felt it was necessary to point out the obvious. "We are kind of on a date right now, aren't we?"

Ben shook his head. "Not exactly. I mean, you had virtually no choice but to come here with me tonight if you wanted to convince your ex that you'd moved on."

"I don't have to convince him," I started. "I have moved on, and he's no longer my concern."

"Right, but if I'd asked you to come with me to this prior to that encounter, would you have agreed?" he challenged.

He had me there. I'd turned him down at the wedding, and I'd done it with such conviction that he knew there was no way I would have even entertained the idea of going to that function with him.

"Fine," I stated, wanting to ignore his question. "I'll give us a chance to get to know one another."

A look of shock broke out on Ben's face. "Really?"

I answered with a smile and a nod.

"Let me guess," he began. "You have a wedding every weekend for the next five months, don't you?"

Shaking my head, I explained, "Actually, I don't. Priscilla and Sebastian's wedding was the last big wedding I had this year. I have one more wedding before the end of the year, and I'm planning for other events like bridal showers. But wedding season is officially over for me."

After a moment of contemplation, Ben decided, "Great. Then, I'm going to pick you up on Saturday afternoon to take you out."

I hadn't expected him to say the afternoon. I figured it'd be dinner out. "Where are we going?" I asked.

"I'm going to take you to see a Broadway show before I take you out to dinner. Afterward, we'll see what happens."

Afterward.

I wanted to bring it up. I wanted to do what Kenzie told me I should do and talk to him about his intentions. But perhaps that was no longer necessary considering he'd made it clear enough with just that one statement.

Regardless, I decided to stick to my word. Ben was charming, really handsome, and a great kisser. I'd give us a chance to get to know one another because I figured that, even in a worst-case scenario, I'd be able to experience more of that. It was hardly a bad trade-off. I'd just be sure to go into this keeping it all in the back of my mind.

If I did that, I'd easily be able to play the part and not get my feelings hurt.

Which is precisely what I was trying to convince myself of at the current moment. If I truly didn't care, I knew I wouldn't have been standing in front of my mirror looking at the outfit I'd decided on for my date with Ben.

An emerald green, three-quarter sleeve, mini dress. It fit snug up top, with a high neckline, and a crisscrossed design of the fabric just beneath my breasts. It landed at mid-thigh, and I paired it with my knee-high brown boots and a brown leather satchel.

Considering this was an afternoon date, I didn't want to go too fancy with my outfit. But since we were having dinner together afterward, I felt it was necessary to put in the effort to dress up a little bit.

When Ben arrived ten minutes later, I met him downstairs instead of buzzing him up. He gave me a hug and a peck on the cheek.

"All set?" he asked.

"Yes," I answered. "Now will you tell me which show we are going to see?"

Ben offered a gorgeous smile before he replied, "My Fair Lady."

I cocked an eyebrow and quizzed him. "Hoping to turn the girl into who you think she should be? What could be better than a girl who will bow to your every whim?"

"You've seen it already?" he frowned.

I shook my head. "No. But that doesn't mean I don't know the story."

"You might know the original, but I've heard this interpretation is impressive. In fact, while it might seem initially that she's the one being controlled, it's not. And in the end, Eliza's the one playing puppeteer."

Interesting.

I never pegged Ben for a Broadway-musical-loving man.

"I'm intrigued," I said softly.

Satisfied with my response, Ben ushered me to his car where he opened my door for me. Twenty minutes later, we were seated in what were the theater's premium seats. Apparently, Ben was sparing no expense for this, even if what was happening between us wasn't meant to be something long-lasting and meaningful.

Not long after, the show started.

I was riveted.

And just under three hours later, it ended. Ben and I waited in our seats while everyone else began filing out. As we sat there, he asked, "So, what did you think?"

"I loved it," I proclaimed. "You definitely heard right. This was an incredible interpretation of it. I was initially worried because Eliza seemed to be playing the part of the object of Henry's subjugation too well. I wasn't totally convinced she'd turn it around. But that ending was utter perfection."

Ben placed his hand on my bare thigh, squeezed, and said, "See what happens when you give something a chance. You never know how things will turn out."

I wanted to focus on the words he was saying, but the feel of his hand on the skin of my leg was distracting me too much.

His thumb stroked back and forth, his eyes watching it move. When he focused his attention on my face again, he instantly pulled his hand away.

"Sorry," he apologized.

While I appreciated the fact that he realized he might have been making me uncomfortable, I didn't want an apology. Because even though his touch had rendered me speechless, I actually liked the way it made me feel.

"It's okay," I assured him.

Ben stared at me a moment before he glanced around the theater. It had emptied out rather quickly, so he looked at me and stated, "It looks like it has thinned out a lot. Are you ready to head to dinner?"

"Yeah."

When we got outside, I asked, "Is it far?"

"The restaurant?" he questioned me.

Nodding, I added, "You didn't say where we were going for dinner. I was just thinking that since we've been sitting for three hours, it might be nice to walk if we're not that far away."

Ben took a minute to think and guessed, "It's probably about a thirty-minute walk from up here near Lincoln Square. If you're up for it, I'm happy to walk. Worst case, we can always catch a cab."

At that, Ben slipped his fingers through mine and guided us away from the theater to Broadway. Once we were on Broadway, we made our way toward Midtown. And we did it with Ben holding my hand the entire time. We talked with one another as we walked, but it was mostly about the play or inconsequential things. I had noticed, however, that we were getting a lot of stares. I could only assume it had to do with Ben having a recognizable face.

Our stroll ended between Forty-Fifth and Forty-Sixth Streets. That's when I looked around and realized where we were having dinner.

The View Restaurant and Lounge.

I'd heard so much about the establishment but never had an opportunity to patronize it.

Glancing up at Ben, I pleaded, "Please tell me we're going to have a window seat."

Ben smiled at me and confirmed, "We're going to have a window seat."

I couldn't stop myself from celebrating. Ben laughed at me and led us into the restaurant. This was going to be my first experience in the only revolving rooftop restaurant in New York. I was beyond excited.

After we'd been seated and had placed our orders, I marveled at the New York City skyline for a few minutes. It was breathtaking.

"Thank you so much for bringing me here," I bubbled. "Between the show and this, it's really been a spectacular day."

Ben was clearly pleased with himself. "I'm glad

you're enjoying yourself, Cora. I'm having a great time with you. It's nice to not only have a break from work but to also spend that time with someone."

Well, there it was.

Someone.

Not necessarily me.

There was no doubt in my mind that Ben could have any woman he wanted. And if the walk from the theater to the restaurant hadn't been enough of an indication of that, the looks we were getting from others inside the restaurant would have solidified it.

Realizing that I'd truly been having a great day, I didn't want to put a damper on it. Instead, I decided to shift the topic to something else he said.

"Can you tell me about your work?" I wondered.

"What do you want to know?"

I shrugged. "Anything. I mean, I only know what I know from hearing about it. It should come as no surprise to you that your name is one that's well-known in this city."

"So, then wouldn't you think you already know everything about me?"

Shaking my head, I assured him, "Absolutely not. Because I've learned a lot about you in the last week. And none of what I've learned from you yourself is anything I've read or heard about you. That tells me that either a lot of that stuff is not accurate, or it's just a small sliver of who you really are."

Ben stared at me for several long moments, contemplating. Suddenly, he sat back in his chair and admitted,

"A lot of what you've read or heard is probably pretty accurate. Not everything, of course, but certainly most of it. That said, it's as you put it. It's really just a small piece of who I am."

"What exactly is it that you do for a living?" I inquired.

"I'm a hedge fund manager."

When he offered no additional explanation, I teased, "I work with brides for a living, so I've got to be honest. I have zero idea what a hedge fund manager does. I know it's got something to do with finance and money, but that's about it."

Our appetizers arrived just as Ben let out a laugh. We both took a few bites before he explained, "I guess the best way to put it is that people, typically very wealthy people who can afford to assume a great amount of risk, trust me to make investment decisions with their money. My investment strategies are generally very aggressive, so there's a lot to be lost if I don't make the right choices. Of course, they stand to gain a lot when I'm right."

I pondered this for a moment. "How much money do you manage if you don't mind me asking?"

"Millions."

"Yeah, nope," I declared. "I'll stick to the Priscillas of the world. Give me a runaway bride, a bridesmaid's dress that needs to be sewed, or a bakery delivery truck broken down on the side of the road any day of the week. I can handle that and not feel an ounce of stress. Being responsible for millions of dollars, a lot of which does not belong to me, is not something I'm ever going to be remotely interested in doing."

Ben let out a full-blown laugh. Seeing it took my breath away.

I managed to recover, so when his laughter died down, I added, "But I commend you for your obvious success with it and your ability to handle that level of stress. I certainly couldn't do it."

Ben shot me a look of indifference. "It's not just you. Honestly, it's not for most people. It requires a lot of hours and a good deal of perseverance. But it really depends on the individual. I don't think it means that what I do is any more difficult than what you do. I could never do what you do."

I smiled. "Now you're just trying to make me feel better."

"No, I'm not," he insisted. "Different jobs just require different types of people to do them. I excel at what I do, but I wouldn't last five minutes dealing with things I'm sure you do."

"Yeah, I guess I have had my fair share of stressful situations to manage over the years," I concurred.

When our food finally arrived, I asked, "Have you lived in the city all your life?"

Ben shook his head. "No. I have a place here now that I stay in during the week since I'm up pretty early and it makes getting to my office much easier. But on the weekends, I typically go to my home in Rosewood."

My brows shot up. Rosewood was a town not far outside of Manhattan. It was one I was intimately familiar with because it was where I'd grown up. "You have two homes?" I asked.

"I only have one home. The other is really just a place to stay during the week."

I loved that. I love that he viewed his place in Rosewood as his real home. Once again, I was reminded of just how little I knew about Ben, and it made me want to get to know him that much more. "I grew up in Rosewood," I shared.

"No kidding?"

My head moved back and forth. "Nope," I answered.

"Did you like it?" he asked.

"Loved it. One day I'll move back, but for now, I'm like you. It's just easier with my job to be right here in the city. And unfortunately for me, I can't afford two separate places," I sighed.

Ben and I continued to eat our dinner and talk. Everything was so effortless that I completely forgot that I should have been keeping my guard up. In the end, I decided it didn't matter. I was having too good of a time to really care.

Ben

Torture.

This was nothing but absolute, pure torture.

I was convinced I'd officially entered Hell.

Today had been an incredible day. Better than I could have ever imagined.

But now I was struggling.

Because Cora and I had arrived back at her place just a little bit ago. She was currently straddling me, her breasts against my chest and her mouth on mine. We'd been kissing like this for easily the last ten minutes. I wasn't sure how much more I could take before I ripped her dress right off her sweet little body.

We'd had such an amazing time today, and I found myself feeling a lot of things I've never felt before. Part of me thought it was because Cora was the first woman I was truly trying to get to know before taking that next step. The other part of me believed that it was the simple fact that it was Cora herself. If it had been anyone else that I'd taken out tonight, I didn't think I'd have been feeling the way I was right now.

There was something about her that was just... different. Between the charity benefit a few days ago and being out with her today, she showed me something I hadn't seen from anyone else before now. She gave me something I wasn't sure I'd ever get from someone when I made the choice to start getting serious about my romantic life.

Her attention.

It was authentic, too.

Cora wasn't concerned with what being with me could do for her social status. In fact, I believed she would have preferred if none of that was part of the equation.

She was genuinely interested in having conversations

with me that were intelligent and meaningful. And I realized that I had made a good choice in pursuing her.

Given the way she was grinding her hips over me now with her lips against mine and her tongue in my mouth, I had to correct myself. Pursuing Cora hadn't been a good choice. It had been a great one. I was convinced of that, and I believed it had the potential to be one of the best decisions of my entire life.

But as great as I believed it could be, right now it was going to cause me a bit of distress. Because Cora was making it very clear that she was enjoying what was happening between us at the moment. And I had little doubt that if I wanted to push this to the next level, she wouldn't deny me.

I made a promise to myself, though.

I wanted more than just a hookup with her. Not only did I need to do things different, but I also wanted to give her what I thought she deserved. So, as much as it pained me to do it given just how hot we both were for one another, I tore my mouth from hers and whispered, "Cora."

Cora rolled her hips over me, her breasts pressing tighter against my chest. "Ben," she rasped.

Fuck.

How was I supposed to deny her? How was I supposed to hear her call my name like that and not do anything about it?

I brought one hand to her hip and gripped it firmly. "Baby, please," I begged. "You've got to slow down for me."

Her body instantly stopped moving as she pulled

back to look at me. I was thankful she did because I had little confidence in my ability to stop it on my own if she didn't. That would have been the opposite of what I wanted. And I knew if we could give ourselves more time to get to know one another, I'd have a greater chance of hearing her say my name like she had for more than just a night.

Despite the relief I felt that Cora had stopped writhing over me, concern and worry littered her features. Seeing that, I almost gave in.

Almost.

Instead, I remembered what I needed to do and suggested, "We should call it a night here."

She blinked in surprise, and her head jerked back just a bit. "Oh," she said softly. "Right. Okay."

Cora started to shift her body to get off of me, but I held her in place. Even though she didn't say anything, I knew what was happening inside her head. And I didn't like what I saw.

"I like this a lot," I started reassuring her. "I like *you* a lot. But there's nothing wrong with us taking some time to get to know one another a little better."

Her brows pulled together. "Really?" she asked.

I dipped my chin. "Yeah."

Cora eyed me suspiciously but didn't question me further. "Okay."

"I'll call you sometime tomorrow. We can make plans to get together again soon. Does that work for you?"

A small smile tugged at her lips before she nodded and confirmed, "Yeah, that works for me."

Giving her hip a squeeze, I replied, "Good. Give me one more kiss before you get up."

At that, Cora leaned forward and gave me another kiss.

And once I got myself in my bed that night, no matter how long the day had been, I found it difficult to find sleep. Because I couldn't think about anything but the promise of Cora.

CHAPTER 6

Cora

"**W**E NEED TO TALK."

"Okay," I replied. "About what?"

"Not over the phone. In person. Today."

I didn't know why it surprised me that I was getting this phone call first thing Monday morning. I should have expected it after this weekend.

"Okay, Kenz. Meet for lunch this afternoon then?" I asked.

My best friend and I worked out the details of our lunch meeting and disconnected.

I got back to work. Or, at least, I tried to.

My mind kept wandering back to the day I'd spent with Ben on Saturday. In a matter of a week, he'd shattered any preconceived ideas I had about him. He'd been charming, attentive, and completely present in our date. Even when I knew people around us were staring, he never seemed to let that bother or distract him. Having that with Ben, I'd realized that it was something I'd been missing with Josh. Something that should have been a huge red flag.

Whenever Josh and I were together, he was on his phone regularly. I had assumed it was all for work. Some of them had been, I guess. But after Ben showed me what it was like to have someone's full focus and attention, it made me wonder how many of Josh's texts and calls he took that caused him to walk out of the room and away from me were actually about work.

Despite that realization, most of my thoughts this morning were about what happened after Ben brought me back home. Our date had been so spectacular, and I was feeling great. I didn't plan to take things all the way with him, but I was a grown woman. I hadn't been with anyone since Josh, even though we'd ended more than a year ago. I'd managed one or two dates, but nothing that amounted to anything special.

Nothing like what I'd had with Ben.

So feeling that spark again, even though I should have been cautious and talked to him first, I pounced instead. Granted, we didn't do much beyond a lot of kissing, but it was still so nice.

Unfortunately, it left me feeling completely distracted today because it was as though I could still feel his lips on mine and his hands moving over my body.

I missed both.

And I wanted more of it all.

But in the back of my mind, the thought still lingered that I might be playing with fire. I had no doubts that when I met with Kenzie later, she'd help me sort it out.

So, I did my best to put thoughts of Ben out of my mind and focus on my work for the rest of the morning.

A few hours later, I was seated at a restaurant waiting for Kenzie. While I waited, I replied to a few emails on my phone.

I'd just pressed send on one when I was startled by a rush of air blowing past my face and the sound of something being slammed down on my table. When I looked up, I saw Kenzie standing there with her eyes narrowed at me.

"What's wrong with you?" I asked.

She pointed her finger down at the table and spat, "That!"

I turned my attention to the table and saw what had her in a tizzy. As shocking as it was for me to see what I was seeing, I wasn't sure I knew why it had her all beside herself.

"I don't even understand how this is possible," I declared, still stunned.

Kenzie slid into the seat across from me. My eyes lifted to hers, and she shared, "I'm trying to figure out how you went from being so concerned about what Ben's intentions were to this."

"What does that mean?"

"Cora, look at your face in these photos!" she all but yelled. "That face screams a whole lot more than caution. In fact, it screams everything *but* caution."

I looked back down at the table. Three different tabloid magazines were spread out before me. On the front cover of each one of them was a photo of Ben and me. Three different photos, but all still the same.

Because in each one of them, I was gazing up at

Ben while on our date Saturday. I had been completely marveling at him as we were walking hand in hand from the theater to the restaurant. I had to admit that Kenzie was right. The look on my face had not an ounce of trepidation.

"I can't believe I'm on the front cover of not one but three tabloids," I murmured.

"There were actually more, but I figured three would do," she informed me.

My eyes widened. I was on the cover of multiple tabloids.

How was this even happening?

The truth was, I didn't even know people had snapped any pictures of us. Though, as evidenced by the photos, it was likely because I hadn't taken my eyes off of Ben long enough to notice. It was then I realized I was like the people in the restaurant and the few I had noticed when we first started walking from the theater. Ben was mesmerizing, and it was hard not to be captivated by him.

Just then, our waitress walked up to the table and took our order. I had been worried she was going to notice the magazines, recognize me, and then ask a million questions. I didn't know what, but I was certain I wouldn't want to answer any of them. Thankfully, she came over, did her job, and walked away.

"This one is my favorite," my friend declared, holding one up. "Not just for the picture either. The headline is everything."

There it was. In bright, bold letters.

New York's most eligible bachelor is off the

market! And just beneath that in smaller print read: **See more photos inside of Benjamin Mason's second date with the mysterious woman.**

"Have you read the article?" I asked.

"Of course," Kenzie confirmed. "Apparently, you're the hottest thing in Manhattan right now because you've managed to score a second date with Ben. Nobody has *ever* gotten a second date with him before now."

"How does anyone know this was our second date?" I wondered.

Kenzie looked at me in disbelief. "My dear friend, you do know who he is, don't you?"

I nodded.

"People make it their business to know everything about him. You two went to the charity event together last week. Photos were taken then, but nobody thought anything of it because it's not uncommon for him to take a date to something like that. The issue is that just two days later he was seen out in public again with the same woman... you."

I shook my head, still trying to come to terms with all of it. "The first one wasn't even a real date," I insisted. "That doesn't count."

"It does to the reporters. And the readers. And, I'm guessing, Ben Mason."

My brows pulled together in confusion. "What do you mean? Why Ben?"

"He likes you, Cora. Why else do you think you're the first woman he's been seen out with twice? That's not how he works."

74

"Okay, so we get along. That doesn't mean that he's suddenly a different man."

"Did you sleep together?" she asked, cutting to the chase.

My eyes widened in shock for a second time. Before I even had a chance to respond, she scolded me, "Don't give me that look of surprise. It's a valid question."

"Not one that the world needs to know the answer to," I noted.

Kenzie's face softened. "I'm not the world. I'm your best friend, and I worry about you. After everything you went through with Josh, I don't want to see you getting hurt again."

"We didn't sleep together," I shared after a beat of silence.

Kenzie visibly relaxed, sitting back in her seat.

"But we did do a lot of kissing," I added.

Kenzie bit the edge of her lip through a smile. "How was it?" she asked.

I took in a deep breath and closed my eyes as I thought again about my night with Ben on my couch. When I opened my eyes, I whispered my reply, "So good."

"Tell me more," she begged.

I finally settled in and gave my friend the details. I filled her in on everything from the moment he showed up until the second he walked out my door. Kenzie didn't interrupt once, though about halfway through my story our food had arrived.

She sat and listened and waited patiently for me to

share every last juicy detail. Once I finished, she just eyed me carefully. I could tell she had a million thoughts running through her brain.

Eventually, she asked, "Have you spoken to him since he left?"

I nodded. "He called me last night. We talked on the phone for nearly two hours before bed. There wasn't any deep conversation, though. It was all just getting-to-know-you stuff."

A grin formed on her face. "Do you have plans to talk to him about where things are between the two of you since you chose not to do it before making out with him?"

I shrugged. "I should have. I know I should have. But we'd been having such a wonderful time, and I kept finding myself surprised by the depth of his character."

"I don't even know what that means," she said.

After taking another deep breath, I explained, "He's not like what I expected. Between Josh and some of the families I deal with for work, I had an idea in my mind about the kind of person Ben would be. He's nothing like that. Sure, he's wealthy and confident. But he doesn't allow his success to go to his head. Ben doesn't assume that he's better than you or me simply because he's wealthier. He treated everyone we encountered with respect. Whenever I used to go out with Josh anywhere, he always seemed to talk down to people. I've yet to see a trace of arrogance in Ben. He works really hard just like everyone else."

I paused a moment to collect my thoughts because I

knew I had to touch on what I had no doubt was at the forefront of Kenzie's mind. "Look, I know there's a lot of speculation and rumors about the kind of person he is. But I honestly believe they simply don't know him at all."

"So, you don't think he's had his fair share of women?" she asked. "I'm not trying to stomp on your parade, but I don't want you blinded by his charm either."

I shook my head. "I'm not. Ben doesn't hide who he is. In fact, he said that a lot of what's been reported about him is true. All I'm saying is that there's a lot more there than people realize."

"Or maybe you're just different for him," she suggested.

"I'd love for that to be true, but what makes me different from anyone else? What is it about me that would make him suddenly want to have more than just one date? Though, like I said before, Saturday was technically only our first date. The charity event didn't count. So, it's still possible that I'm not any different and won't get more than just the one that I did."

Kenzie took a sip of her drink. After she put it back on the table, with a puzzled look, she wondered, "You mean you didn't set up another date?"

"No," I told her.

"Not even when he called you last night?" she pressed.

"No," I repeated.

Looking more than just slightly perplexed, she asked, "Do you think he's going to ask for another date?"

I shrugged. Even though I sincerely hoped there

would be another date, I had no idea if Ben wanted one. Obviously, yesterday's phone call led me to believe he was still interested after our date Saturday, but the fact that he hadn't talked about getting together again left me wondering.

"Cora?" Kenzie called.

"Yeah?"

"Do you want another date with him?" she asked.

Nodding, I added softly, "I want more than just another date with him."

Glancing down at her phone to check the time, Kenzie said, "Okay. I don't have much time before I have to go and get back to work. Here's the deal. If he calls you again and asks for another date, you should go. But you need to find a way to somehow talk to him about where you are. Your heart is fragile, Cora. He seems like he's been decent enough with you up to this point. If you share that, it will at least give him the opportunity to be forthcoming with what's in his head."

"That's all I want," I stated. "I don't expect promises of forever. I mean, I just met the guy. But I'd like to know that this is something a bit more serious for him. It wouldn't feel good to know I was just another woman to add to his list."

"I don't think you will be," she insisted. "But you've got to talk to him. Do it before you let him kiss you so your mind doesn't get all muddled."

I laughed. "I'll try to remember that."

Kenzie and I sat for a few more minutes talking about work-related things while we waited for the check, but she had to leave right afterward. We parted ways at the entrance. She took off in one direction; I went in the other with the tabloids tucked up under my arm.

My lunch with Kenzie, with its addition of photographic evidence of my raptured state of mind, helped me realize a few things. The first was that if I wanted to make it through whatever was happening with Ben with my heart in one piece, I needed to do what I'd been saying from the start. I had to be cautious and upfront with him.

Of course, in realizing that that was going to be the next step, it suddenly hit me that Ben might give me an answer I didn't want to hear. And while I wanted him to be honest and would rather know upfront, the thought that he might not want to pursue something more serious with me was disappointing.

I found it crazy that I was even in this position. Just over a week earlier I had been dreading the fact that I was not only pulled into a wedding as a last-minute emergency but also that I'd managed to end up paired with him. I hadn't wanted anything to do with him. And yet, now that I'd had an opportunity to really get to know him, it worried me that I might not get the chance to see if this could really be something more.

When I arrived back at my office, I got back to work. I was far more productive that afternoon than I had been that morning. Spending hours working on a couple different projects, by the time I was ready to leave for the day, I'd gotten more accomplished than I'd originally planned.

Later that night, after I'd gone home and had dinner, Ben called.

"Hey, baby, how was your day today?" he greeted me.

Baby.

"Good," I replied. "I got a lot done and even managed to have lunch with Kenzie."

Ben knew that Kenzie was my best friend because I'd told him about her when we talked on the phone last night.

"That's good. So, all's well in the wedding world then," he stated, clearly indicating he believed I had everything under control.

"It is. And how's the world of finance starting the week? Was your day productive?" I asked.

Ben let out a laugh. "Everything is great there. I have a heck of a week ahead of me, though. I'm expecting long work hours for the next several days because not only do I have my normal workload, but I'm also trying to land another big client this week. It'll be huge if I can finesse it."

"Well, you're very good at what you do, so if they decide not to work with you, it's their loss," I insisted.

"I appreciate the vote of confidence. Anyway, I still have a lot of work to get done before tomorrow, but I wanted to see how your day was and ask you if you'd be able to get together this weekend."

A second real date.

This was a big deal. Maybe there was something different about me. I wanted that to be true, but also knew

I needed to talk to him about it before things when much further. So, I responded, "I would love to get together this weekend."

I could hear the smile in his voice when he replied, "Will Friday evening work for you?"

"Yes."

"Great," he replied. "I'll pick you up around six."

"Can't wait," I shared.

With that, Ben and I disconnected. Then, I spent the rest of the night trying not to get excited about the fact that perhaps this thing with Ben had the potential to be more than just a fling for him.

CHAPTER 7

Cora

"THERE ARE JUST UNDER TWO WEEKS LEFT," I offered information that my soon-to-be bride, Julia, already knew.

"I know," she immediately replied. "I'm kind of freaking out."

This was not an unusual occurrence in any wedding that I planned. Something about that two-week mark seemed to put everyone on edge. I expected it and made it a point to communicate frequently with my clients to keep their minds at ease.

Knowing we'd reached that point with Julia, I came into work this morning and made a bunch of calls that I didn't get to yesterday. I worked through until lunchtime making sure everything was in order. Now that I'd just finished lunch, I figured it was time to reach out to the bride.

"Well, this call should help you freak out just a little less then," I assured her.

"I don't know if that's possible," Julia doubted me.

I couldn't help but smile. It was always the same, and over the years, I'd learned to perfect the art of cool in situations like this.

"Alright, let me at least try," I pretended to plead with her.

"Okay. Honestly, it can't hurt. I doubt it's possible to feel any worse than I already do," she murmured.

"Right. First things first, I've already been in touch with the photographer, videographer, deejay, makeup artist, florist, limo service, and pastor," I began. "Everyone knows where they need to be, what they need to have, and what time. I also contacted the venue for the reception and confirmed they received the document I emailed over to them with the final headcount and food selections. Everything is all set there as well."

"What about the singer for the ceremony?" she began to fret.

"I called her this morning and left a voicemail," I began. "She teaches during the day, so I suspect I won't hear back from her until sometime later this afternoon."

There was a moment of hesitation before Julia worried, "Oh wait. The centerpieces and favors. Are they ready?"

The poor girl was a nervous wreck. I felt bad for her. She and her fiancé lived in the city, but none of their family and friends did. In fact, most of them didn't even live in New York. This meant that without having anyone close by to help with the details, Julia had to hire me. She had a lovely group of friends who'd stand up for her on the big day and had planned her bridal shower and bachelorette party, but they weren't around to deal with the important things that might get overlooked otherwise.

"I just finished up the centerpieces late last week and delivered them to the venue. While I was there, I instructed the events manager on what needed to be done with them once the florist delivered the rose petals, so they're all set. This week, I'll be working on finishing up the favors. I'm already about halfway through on those."

"You weren't lying," Julia stated. "I actually do feel a little bit better now."

I rolled my eyes as I smiled and shook my head. Every. Single. Time.

"I'm happy to hear that. I'll reach out to you as soon as I've finished up your favors and once I hear from the singer. Other than that, you just do what you've got to do to make sure you stay as relaxed as possible. I'm good at what I do, and your makeup artist is phenomenal, but stress acne isn't something with which anybody wants to deal. If you need a place to unload any of your stress, give me a call and we'll work through it. Okay?"

"Okay. Thanks, Cora. I don't know what I would have done without all of your help," she sighed.

"You're welcome."

Julia and I disconnected. Then, as promised, I got to work on her favors. I spent the rest of my day getting another quarter of them done. I called it quits just before dinner and decided I'd come in first thing tomorrow morning to finish them up. On my walk back to my apartment, I got a call from the singer. We confirmed details, and I sent a text to Julia letting her know that was one less thing for her to stress about.

When she replied that she'd been slightly panicked all afternoon about it, all I could do was shake my head and smile.

With the work I had been doing preparing all of the last few details for Julia's wedding, the week flew by. It was finally Friday afternoon, and I was so excited about being able to see Ben for the first time in nearly a whole week.

Despite how busy we both were, we'd still managed to communicate with each other throughout the week. Other than the time he called me on Tuesday, we hadn't spoken. But we sent texts back and forth to one another.

And some of them had my heart skipping a beat.

On Wednesday night, it was difficult to find sleep because of the text he sent me mid-morning out of the blue.

Miss you, baby. Looking forward to seeing you on Friday.

Maybe it wasn't anything spectacular, but it felt nice to know that I was on his mind. I sent him a reply expressing the same. Once I finished up Julia's favors, I snapped a picture and sent it to him, explaining that I'd been finding ways to keep myself busy.

On Thursday, when I decided to get ahead of the

game and start researching some ideas for an upcoming bachelorette party early next year, I sent him a fun text.

I get that you work with lots of money all the time, but surely you can't be having as much fun as me. I'm currently deciding whether it's better to get molds for a bunch of smaller chocolate penises or one large one. Decisions, decisions. ☺

Ben didn't respond immediately, and I started to wonder if perhaps I'd crossed a line. Thankfully, when he replied about an hour later, he didn't seem the least bit bothered.

What kind of size difference are we talking about here?

I responded instantly. **The small ones are only two inches long. The large one is just over eight inches.**

Ben: **Wait. Are you seriously unsure which is better?**

Me: **Yes! Because these are likely going to be made into lollipops.**

Ben: **Okay, that still shouldn't be a question.**

Me: **Ben. The problem isn't necessarily going to be about putting them inside one's mouth. I'd have to find sticks to support the weight of the larger ones.**

Ben: **Fuck. I shouldn't be discussing this with you right now. I have to get on a call in a few minutes.**

Me: **Hahaha. Okay, I'll let you go. In the meantime, maybe I'll order one of each and test them out.**

Ben: **And here I thought I was the one who'd be trouble...**

I simply replied with an angel emoji.

Ben didn't respond immediately, but he did end up reaching out that night. We didn't nearly have the same playful communication as we did earlier in the day; however, just knowing he was taking the time out to touch base with me was nice.

And now, after nearly a week had passed since I'd last seen him, it was finally here. I couldn't wait to see Ben again. I went into work early this morning and worked through lunch. Shortly afterward, I decided to call it quits for the day and went home ahead of my normal end time.

No sooner did I walk through the door of my apartment, though, when my phone rang. Pulling it out of my bag, I saw Ben's name on the display.

"Hey you!" I greeted him.

"Hi, Cora. I'm so sorry about this, but I'm not going to be able to pick you up like we originally planned. At the last minute, we had to schedule a meeting with the new potential client. The meeting isn't until five o'clock, so it'll give me enough time between when my regular workday ends and then to run home, shower, and grab some clothes. I'll head back to my office and have my meeting, but I probably won't be done until closer to six. Our reservations are for six-thirty. I tried to have my assistant move dinner back, but they don't have anything else open later."

I'd been looking forward to seeing him all week. This was crushing and disappointing news. "Oh," I mumbled, unsure of what else to say.

"I still want to see you, Cora," he assured me. "I was

just curious if there would be any way you could meet me here at my office? Like I said, I don't think I'll be much later than six, so we should still be able to make our reservation on time if you can do that."

Relief swept through me.

"Of course. I'll just need the address."

There was a pause before he asked, "You don't know where my office is?"

"No," I answered honestly. "Should I? I mean, it's not like I'm going to become one of your clients any time soon."

Through his laughter, Ben replied, "You always manage to surprise me, baby."

"I try."

Ben gave me the address to his office before we disconnected. I took my time over the next few hours getting myself ready. With time to spare, I decided not to rush the process. The last thing I wanted was to show up at Ben's office looking frazzled.

When it was finally time, I walked out of my apartment and grabbed a taxi to head toward the finance district. Once I entered the building and gave my name, I was directed to the elevator. I rode up the glamorous elevator and stepped out when the doors opened on Ben's floor. Stepping through the glass doors immediately off the elevator, I walked in to find two women, a significant age gap between them, sitting behind a reception desk.

The older woman greeted me first. "Hi, how can I help you?" she asked.

"My name is Cora Daniels. I'm actually here to meet Ben," I told her.

"Oh, that's right," she exclaimed. "He mentioned that, but we've been so busy it slipped my mind. He's still in his meeting, but if you want to have a seat over there, I'm sure he'll be out soon."

I looked in the direction she was pointing. When I turned my attention back to her, I said, "Thank you."

"Of course."

"Can we get you anything to drink while you wait?" the younger woman asked.

I shook my head. "No, thank you. I'm alright."

With that, I walked over to the reception lounge and looked around. I couldn't call it a waiting room because that wouldn't suffice. This was, without a doubt, a lounge. The entire space screamed class and sophistication. It was bright, open, and looked out into the New York City streets. To top it off, because Ben's company was located on one of the top floors of the sky-rise building, it had an incredible view of the city's skyline.

I picked up a magazine from the coffee table, but after I flipped through a few pages of the finance magazine that I found not even the slightest bit interesting, I put it back down. As I sat there, I couldn't help but overhear part of the conversation between the two women at the reception desk. From what I could tell, the older one was training the younger one. I was surprised that they were still here this late on a Friday evening, though.

The time ticked by, but Ben never emerged from wherever his personal office was. I distracted myself from the worry that we were going to miss our dinner reservations by pulling out my phone and scrolling through social media and checking my emails.

It was when I heard two people laughing that I lifted my gaze from my phone. The laughter was not from the two receptionists, who had since left.

No.

It was from a man and a woman.

That man was Ben.

And he was walking out behind an incredibly beautiful woman, who was dressed to the nines. I had to admit she had great style, but I couldn't do much beyond that. I was completely frozen to the chair, not making a single sound or movement. Ben glanced in my direction for a brief moment and gave me a smile along with his panty-melting wink before he turned his attention back to the woman who hadn't noticed me.

When she stopped walking just inside the front glass door, she turned and smiled at Ben.

"Thank you for being so accommodating and meeting me tonight," she said. But it was the sound of her voice that grated my nerves. Because it was all about seduction and sultriness. I couldn't have managed to pull off a voice like that if I tried.

"It's not a problem, Lisa. We aim to provide a level of service and satisfaction that you won't find anywhere else. We're happy to have you on board," Ben returned.

This was the client he'd been working so hard all week to land? I thought.

I watched as Lisa looked at Ben. She wasn't hiding

her attraction to him very well, and I cringed at the thought that perhaps they'd slept together at some point.

"Are you sure you don't want to join me for a drink?" she asked.

Ben smiled at her but gave a gentle shake of his head. "I'm sorry, Lisa. But tonight's not a good night."

Tonight's not? Did that mean another night would be?

Lisa didn't hide her disappointment. Nevertheless, she gave him a nod and ended, "Right. Well, maybe another time then. Thanks again, Ben."

Ben reached around her and opened the door. "I'll be in touch next week," he stated as she walked out.

The minute he pulled the door closed, he reached up and locked it. Then, he turned in my direction. In an instant, he went from having a smile on his face to pure concern. It was then, I believed, he made an assumption about my state of mind.

Walking in my direction, he lamented, "I'm so sorry about that, Cora. I truly did not expect it would take that long."

I gave him a slow nod of understanding even though it killed me to do so. "It's fine," I responded, hoping I sounded convincing.

When Ben stopped in front of me, he held his hand out. I placed my hand in his and stood. I was barely on my feet for a second when Ben slid his arms around me and pulled me in for a hug. He pressed a kiss to my forehead and said, "Missed you."

"Mm," I replied, still unable to really formulate any coherent response that wouldn't make me sound catty.

With his arms still around me, Ben went on, "We missed our reservation."

"Yep."

"You look amazing."

Of course, I did. I went through the trouble to make myself look amazing. I had on my black faux leather pants, a black satin camisole that had a lace-trimmed V that started at the strap and went down to my bellybutton. I paired it with a cute jacket and a pair of black, patent-leather pumps.

"Thanks," I answered.

"If it's alright with you, I'd like to take you back to my place so I can make it up to you," he declared.

My body tensed. "Make it up to me?" I wondered.

Ben began laughing. "Yes, Cora. I'll make dinner for you to make up for the fact that I not only kept you here waiting all this time but also caused us to miss our dinner reservation. What did you think I meant?"

I took a step back from him, looked in his eyes, and cocked an eyebrow. Otherwise, I gave him no response to his question.

Ben grinned and teased, "You're thinking about having sex with me, aren't you?"

My jaw dropped as shock registered on my face. "I am not!" I asserted.

"I've been thinking about it," he claimed, causing me to snap my lips together. "With you, of course." When I kept my mouth closed, he continued, "But I was really just referring to making you dinner tonight."

I didn't know what to do.

That's wrong.

My body wanted me to go to Ben's for dinner and admit to him afterward that I had been thinking about sex with him. But my brain was telling me that it might not be such a good idea because if I followed through on that, I'd do exactly what Kenzie said I shouldn't. My mind would be muddled, and I'd never talk to Ben about what I needed if this was going to be a serious thing.

"Considering we missed our reservation, the fact that I'm hungry, and that it's after six-thirty on a Friday night in Manhattan where we won't be able to get another reservation for hours, I'll allow you to take me back to your place so you can make dinner for me," I acquiesced.

"Wow. All the stars had to align for you to agree to having me cook for you. I thought most women would be happy that a man wanted to do that for them," he reasoned.

Yeah, I'll bet Lisa would have been all over that, I thought.

My eyes narrowed at him. "I'm not most women."

There was a gleam in his eye and a grin on his face when his voice dropped an octave, and he claimed, "Oh, I know that. Without a doubt, you're most definitely not like most women."

With that, Ben linked his fingers with mine and led me back to his personal office where he grabbed his keys and cell phone. He didn't give me an opportunity to really take in his space because no sooner had we walked in when we were walking back out again.

Five minutes later, we were in his car on the way back to his place. I used the silent drive back to try and pull my thoughts together. If I wanted to avoid a situation like what happened only moments ago in his office with Lisa from being able to wreck me, I had to figure out how I was going to bring it up to him.

But by the time we arrived at his place, I wasn't sure I'd come up with anything good.

CHAPTER 8

Cora

"**S**O, DID YOU FIGURE IT OUT?"

I looked at Ben, who was currently standing on the opposite side of the kitchen island cleaning up from dinner, and asked, "Figure what out?"

"Your dilemma with the chocolate dicks," he clarified. "I was just curious if you'd done any official research yet."

I gave him a disbelieving look. "Suddenly you're okay discussing this with me?"

"I wasn't ever not okay discussing it," he insisted. "The timing just wasn't exactly ideal. Do you know what it was like for me to go into that call after I got those texts from you? I couldn't stop thinking about you talking to me like that."

I jerked my head back and worried, "Did I offend you?"

Now it was Ben's turn to give me an incredulous look. "Are you seriously asking me that question? Do you honestly believe that I'd have brought it up just now if it offended me?"

I shrugged. "I guess not."

Ben continued to load dishes into the dishwasher as a moment of silence stretched between us. "Well?" he prompted.

"Well, what?"

"Did you figure it out?" he repeated his earlier question.

With a look of uncertainty, I disclosed, "The jury is still out. But the supplies for testing are on their way."

"You'll keep me updated, right?"

Smiling, I assured him, "Of course."

Ben gave me an approving nod and returned his attention back to the task at hand. Considering he'd managed to find a way to talk to me about something from my week, I figured it was necessary for me to do the same. Unfortunately, the one thing that he spoke about all week was the big account he was hoping to land. That meant I was going to have to bring up Lisa.

"Um, I hope you don't think I was eavesdropping, but it was kind of hard not to hear. Would I be correct to assume that your meeting tonight was about the big account you've been stressed about all week?"

"You would be correct," he declared.

"And it sounded like you got the account," I continued.

"I did," he confirmed.

A big part of me was truly happy for him, so I couldn't help myself from sharing that. "Congratulations," I praised him. But because the other part of me secretly didn't like Lisa for the simple fact that she was beautiful, had been alone with Ben when we were supposed to be having dinner, and that she didn't even try to hide that she was into him, I added, "I honestly don't understand why you were even worried."

"I wouldn't say I was worried," he corrected me. "I was trying to be positive, while also remaining realistic. There was no guarantee that we'd land the account."

"Well, if Lisa is the woman who owned the account, I'm telling you that you really had nothing to worry about."

Confusion washed over him. "What do you mean?" he asked.

I laughed. When I looked at Ben, I realized he genuinely had no idea what I was getting at. I wiped the smile off my face and explained, "That woman has got it bad for you."

"What? No, she doesn't," he disputed.

I rolled my eyes. "Oh, please. Don't act like you don't know."

"I don't," he deadpanned.

Taking in the seriousness of his face, I realized that perhaps Ben didn't realize. Either that, or he was doing a really good job of faking it. "What time does work usually end on Friday?"

"What?"

"Just answer," I encouraged him.

Ben hesitated briefly, but ultimately replied, "The stock exchange closes at four. Generally, my staff is at the office for thirty minutes to an hour beyond that."

"Based on what I heard her say while I was sitting

there, it is clear to me that she requested the late Friday appointment with you. It's likely she knows what landing her account means for your business and knew she could probably end up in that office alone with you. I saw the way she looked at you. Trust me, that woman wants you."

Ben held my eyes a moment. When he spoke, he defended her. "Cora, Lisa is married."

I tilted my head to the side, pursed my lips, and claimed, "She's not happy in her marriage."

Ben didn't reply. His disbelief was plain as day, so I went on, "My job is being around married people or very soon-to-be-married people. I know how people who are happily married behave, even the rich ones. Lisa is not one of them."

When Ben still made no move to respond, I began wondering what was running through his mind. Was he suddenly realizing that this rich, beautiful woman did have the hots for him? I didn't know what she did for a living, but she was obviously extremely wealthy. If she and Ben ever got together, they could probably rule the world.

Starting to grow uncomfortable with the turn things had taken, I figured it was best to try and redirect the conversation elsewhere. "What does she do anyway?" I wondered.

"As it is, I've probably already said more than I should have about my client," Ben began. "I really can't continue this conversation."

That was like taking a knife to the gut. "Right, sorry.

That was rude of me," I admitted. Even though I understood he had to respect the privacy of his clients, my shoulders fell and my gaze dropped to my lap.

Seconds later, I felt Ben's presence at my side. His forefinger gently touched the skin under my chin and lifted. When my gaze caught his, he asked, "What's happening here?"

"What do you mean?"

"Dinner was great. We talked, laughed, and had a great time. Beyond that, talking about your work-related dilemma was fine. Then, the conversation turned to my work and my new client. It was fine and you were confident in what you were saying. But the minute I said we can't discuss specifics, the mood of the evening completely changed. Why?"

I guessed now was as good of a time as any.

"It's not about you being unable to discuss specifics," I assured him. "I understand there are privacy laws. It's just..." I trailed off, unsure of how to bring it up. Suddenly, I blurted, "Do you read the tabloids?"

Ben jerked his head in surprise at the sudden change in topic. I wasn't sure if this was the way to do this, but it's what came out of my mouth, so I was running with it.

"Not exactly," he replied.

"I didn't think so," I claimed.

"What do the tabloids have to do with anything?" he asked.

I took in a deep breath and blurted, "I don't want to be the stupid girl."

He blinked his eyes at me, clearly trying to figure out what that meant. I saved him the trouble and quickly added, "There were at least three different tabloids that had pictures of you and me from our date last weekend on the front cover."

Ben's face softened. "Cora, I'm sorry. I am so accustomed to my picture being taken that I didn't even think about it. We can find ways to be more discreet if it bothers you."

I shook my head. "It's not that, Ben. It was more about what the headlines said that triggered some feelings inside me."

Ben moved around the counter, added some wine to my glass, and grabbed his own before he took me by the hand and led me over to the huge sectional. Once we were seated, he turned toward me and asked, "What did they say?"

"Summing it up? Basically, that the city's most eligible bachelor is off the market."

His brows pulled together. "And this is a problem?"

Um...

Was he saying...

"I don't... well, are you?" I stammered.

"What do you think?" he challenged.

Shaking my head, I admitted, "I honestly don't know. All I know is I don't want to be that girl who makes assumptions about what's happening between us only to realize down the road that what I thought isn't actually the way it is."

Ben covered my hand with his and stroked his thumb

along my knuckles. "I don't know where you stand, Cora. I know where I am, and I know what I want. My best guess based on last weekend, especially how it ended, and everything between us this week leading up to right now tells me that there's at least a mutual attraction."

He wasn't wrong about that. But it still wasn't enough for me to be sure that I was the only one he was interested in.

"I feel like what I just said doesn't help you at all," he cut into my thoughts.

I took a deep breath and let it out slowly. "I hope you don't take any offense to this, but you've not exactly been portrayed as the kind of guy who sticks to one woman for very long. In fact, the big buzz was all about the fact that we were being seen together on a second date. Obviously, you and I both know that the first time we went out together wasn't real, but my friend made me realize that the reporters don't exactly know that."

Now, it was Ben's turn to sigh. "I'm a bit disappointed you don't think that going to the charity event was more than just a show for your ex. Maybe it started that way, but from the moment I kissed you in that café, it wasn't like that for me at all."

My eyes widened in surprise.

"Why does that shock you?" he wondered.

"Because I'm so confused. This is out of character for you," I told him.

"What is?"

I lifted my hand and waved it between us. "This. You and me and more than just one date," I explained.

"Look, I realize I don't exactly have the best reputation when it comes to that. I'm not going to lie and pretend that the reporters haven't at least been accurate as far as that goes. But the truth is, I lived a long time believing that I'd gotten everything I wanted in life. Success, wealth, family, and friends. And with all that came women. Looking at it now, I'm not exactly proud of that part of my life. But I can't change it. A few weeks before Sebastian and Priscilla's wedding, I started thinking a lot about where I want to end up in life. Meaningless hookups aren't part of that equation anymore. So, yeah, I guess this is out of character for me. But I hope that just because it is doesn't mean that you don't believe I don't actually like or want what's developing between us."

I just stared at him, unable to respond. I hadn't expected this explanation from him. He was mentioning his family and friends for the very first time, which threw me. But it was hearing that he had decided to make a change in his life to go after something he wanted. Something that might be a little more permanent. That's what caused a bunch of nerves to form in my belly.

Ben used my silence as his opportunity to ask, "What assumption do you believe you're going to make about us that's going to be wrong?"

"I guess there are two that sort of go hand in hand. I'm worried that I'm going to think this is something special and meaningful. With that, I'll assume exclusivity exists between us. And I'm not really keen on jumping into something like that again where the other person isn't on the same page."

"So what you're saying is, you want me all to yourself," Ben teased. He was smiling, so I knew he was just trying to lighten the mood, but I knew I couldn't allow myself to be fooled by his charm.

I kept my tone low and serious when I answered, "Not if that's the opposite of what you want."

Ben was thrown by my response and studied me.

I added, "That doesn't mean I'm willing to be just another body in your bed when it's convenient for you. I'm bringing this up now because I have to bring it up. It's only been a week since our date, but I already have feelings for you. I know that with a little bit of time, it won't be hard for me to fall for you, too. After going through what I did in my last relationship, I know what I can handle. And being one of many is not something I can handle."

I paused a moment, took in the look on his face, and continued, "If that's what this was going to be for you, Ben, it's okay. You are who you are. But I know who I am. And it's more important for me to have this be awkward now to save myself the heartache. I promise if that's what this was for you, there are no hard feelings. I need to know now, though, because at least I can still walk away before my heart gets involved more than it already is."

Ben reached out and took the wine glass from my hand. After setting it down on the coffee table, he shifted his body closer to mine. He cupped my face in his hands, and I felt his thumbs stroke along my cheeks. "This is something special, Cora," he started. "You are someone special. And you're not going to be one of many. I can't make promises about where this will end up, but I can make you that promise. For as long as it's us, it'll be just us."

I could feel my throat getting tight with all the emotions I was feeling. Even still, I managed to squeak out, "Are you sure?"

Without hesitating, Ben replied, "Yes."

"You scare me," I admitted.

"Why?"

"Because I still don't understand," I rasped.

His face moved closer to mine. "Understand what, baby?"

I took a moment to reply, but when I did, I whispered, "Why me?"

CHAPTER 9

Ben

WHY HER? How Cora could even ask a question like that was beyond me. She was an incredible woman that I was really beginning to adore. Truthfully, I couldn't imagine it being anyone else I'd been with before her.

This whole conversation had really done a number on me. I tried not to let it show, but there were moments that I felt so much, I couldn't even respond to Cora. One of those moments had been when she admitted that she had feelings for me and that her heart was already involved.

The way I'd been handling this thing with Cora was new to me. For that reason, I didn't know just how much of what I was feeling was typical. It had been worrying me over the last week the frequency with which I thought about her. Not once had I ever missed a woman like that. In fact, I hadn't ever missed a woman like that at all.

So, Cora's admission that she was feeling something

for me was a huge relief. Because at least I knew I wasn't alone in it.

On the other hand, some of what she expressed to me made me feel like perhaps I should walk away from her. When she brought up the reason for her justifiable concern—the fact that I'd never really been serious with one woman before her—it stung a little. Because I had looked at myself as being better than her ex. I thought he had been such a fool for cheating on her with other women when she was under the impression they were exclusive.

But I began wondering if I was just being a hypocrite. The only thing that made me feel like I had a bit of an edge over him was the fact that I'd never given any woman the impression that there was anything serious between us. I never pretended to be in a committed relationship only to go out and fool around behind someone's back.

It was safe to assume that I was a mix of emotions about everything surrounding what I had with Cora. And right now, holding her face in my hands, having listened to the trepidation in her tone as she whispered her question, I knew I had to find a way to give her something meaningful and honest.

"Why you?" I asked.

She gave one gentle downward jerk of her chin in response.

"Cora, baby, why not you?" I retorted. "You're unlike any woman I've ever met. I'll admit that when I first met you on the road beside that broken down delivery truck, it was all about your physical beauty for me. You're gorgeous; you've got to know that. But then there was the wedding, the dance, the kissing in the café, the dress you wore to the charity event, your sarcasm, the joy on your face when we spent the day together last weekend, the kissing on your couch afterward, talking on the phone for hours the next day, and getting sweet, funny, or unexpected texts all week long from you."

I saw the wetness gathering in her eyes. Even still, I didn't stop.

"But the best thing about you is how you see me," I started again. "And I'm not talking about tabloid reports. You knew who I was from the very beginning, and yet you didn't jump at the opportunity to go on a date or get to know me better. If I'd have asked any other woman to spend time with me after that wedding, and she knew who I was, she would have never walked away. You did. You aren't interested in me simply because I have money, Cora. Honestly, I think you'd like me more if I didn't have so much."

Cora bit the corner of her lip to stop herself from smiling through the tears welling in her eyes. I knew I'd hit the nail on the head with that one.

"You have feelings for me that are all about me, not my money. I love that. Never have I ever had that. That's special, and it's not something I want to risk letting go of just so I can have a meaningless hookup with someone else. So, it's all of that, Cora. All of that and whatever else is to come is why it's you."

"Ben?" she whispered.

"Yeah, baby?"

"Kiss me," she ordered.

The desperation in her voice left me with no other choice but to give her what she wanted.

I crushed my mouth to hers and kissed her. Her hands, which had been wrapped around my forearms, moved to my shoulders. And the moment our tongues touched, she moaned. My hands left her face, one going behind her head, the other around her waist.

We kissed a long time before Cora pressed her hands to my chest and pushed me away. Our mouths disconnected, and I had the chance to look at her lust-filled face. Damn, she was beautiful.

Cora wasted no time in crawling toward me, straddling my lap, and kissing me again. Within seconds, she was pulling her jacket down her arms. Underneath that jacket was a loose-fitting satin and lace top. With its low neckline and thin straps, so much of Cora's skin was exposed. I couldn't stop myself from burying my face in her neck.

Then, my mouth was moving over her skin, from her neck to her bare shoulders and back. Cora had her hands in my hair as she rolled her hips and ground down on my cock.

"Ben," she rasped.

I kissed up her throat and over to her ear. When I sunk my teeth gently onto her earlobe, she begged, "Ben, please."

"Tell me what you want, Cora."

With her seductive eyes and hoarse voice, she pleaded, "More."

The second the word had slid past her lips, I captured her mouth again. As we kissed, I slipped my fingers under the thin, delicate straps of her top. I began sliding them down her arms until I stopped at her elbows.

Cora tore her mouth from mine and pulled back just far enough for me to take in the sight of her naked breasts. Closing my mouth over one nipple, I brought my hand up and cupped her other breast. My tongue flicked over the hardened peak in my mouth while my thumb stroked over the other one in my hand.

Cora moaned louder and moved her hips faster.

I switched sides and sucked her other nipple into my mouth while Cora pulled at my shirt. When she managed to pull it up far enough, I reluctantly released her breast from my mouth. After my shirt was gone, Cora put her hands to my shoulders and pushed me until my back was against the couch, my mouth too far away from her body.

Looking up at her, I saw the desire in her eyes. She began scooting her hips backward so she could angle herself and start exploring my body. Her lips roamed over my shoulders and chest. I heard her feet hit the floor as her palms went on a southward journey over the skin of my torso.

The next thing I knew, Cora was kneeling in front of me with her fingers working at the fly of my jeans. No sooner did she lower the zipper when she gripped the waistband and began yanking them down, taking my boxer briefs with them.

Once she'd removed everything, her eyes hit the prize.

Cora wrapped one hand around the base of my cock and looked up at me through gleaming eyes when she brought the tip to her mouth and moistened it with her tongue. I had about a second to regain some control before she took me inside her mouth. And the enthusiasm of what she did next caught me off guard.

Cora did not hold back. She sucked, licked, and stroked with such a hunger, I had no idea how I stopped myself from coming. I let her continue for as long as I could, but refused to let her see me through to the end without making sure she was taken care of first.

"Cora, baby," I called after I'd given her as much time as I could to have her fun.

She drew her mouth back slowly over my length, and her eyes caught mine. After she pressed a kiss to the tip, she replied with a breathy, "Yeah?"

I grinned and answered, "My turn."

As I stood, I lifted her from her knees. Once she was standing in front of me, I picked her up. She wrapped her legs around my waist as I led us to my bedroom. The entire way there, Cora's mouth continued to run over my skin.

The minute her back hit the bed, I pulled off her shoes while she unbuttoned her pants. She started pushing them down her legs, but I quickly took over and pulled them from her body. Then, I parted her legs and tasted her.

Divine.

She tasted magnificent.

Licking. Sucking. Devouring.

I didn't know what it was, but something had changed for me with Cora. And right now, I wanted all I could get of her.

Her taste.

Her sound.

Her touch.

Cora ground her pussy down harder against my mouth. My eyes opened and looked up to see one of her hands gripping the comforter while the fingers of her other hand were toying with one of her nipples.

Seeing that, I couldn't stop the groan that escaped me.

"Ben," Cora breathed.

I didn't relent. My tongue moved faster, plunging inside her for every last bit. That was all it took. Within seconds, Cora moaned as the pleasure tore through her.

I saw her through her orgasm before I began kissing my way up her body.

"You're incredible," she whispered against my lips.

I grinned and promised, "That was nothing, baby."

A lazy, sated smile spread across her face. "How about you show me what I'm missing then?" she challenged.

I gave her a kiss before I leaned over to the bedside table and grabbed a condom from the drawer. As I rolled it on, I looked down at the beautiful woman in my bed. She was like nobody I'd ever been with before, and I had no doubt that something extraordinary was about to happen.

Just as I was about to settle myself between Cora's parted thighs, she moved. She was up on her knees in front of me, putting her hands to my shoulders.

"I've changed my mind," she declared. "It's my turn. You'll have to show me what you've got later."

Later, I thought.

I didn't have a problem with later.

"Taking charge?" I asked.

She nodded.

"I'm used to being the boss, though," I noted.

Urging me back on the bed, Cora pointed out, "You're not the only one."

I loved seeing this feisty side of her. I'd enjoyed it when we were fully clothed, so knowing she had this in her in the bedroom made the promise of her even sweeter.

I fell to my back, and Cora almost instantly straddled me. No sooner did I place my hands on her thighs, when I felt her positioning me at her entrance. Then, I watched as she lowered herself onto my shaft.

My fingers dug into the flesh of her thighs as my eyes roamed over her body, ultimately finding her gaze on me. She stayed there, staring and unmoving, for several long, torturous seconds.

"Cora?" I called.

"Hm?"

"Baby, you've got to play the part of boss right now, or I'm going to have to fire you and assume the role myself," I warned her.

She managed to snap out of her daze and began moving. Cora did not disappoint either. I'd always been the one in charge in the bedroom, so I was a little worried that this wouldn't do it for me.

But it did.

It did that and so much more.

Cora decided she wanted to be the boss in the bedroom, and she was taking the role seriously. This wasn't the typical corporate world. She didn't expect someone else to do the work that she'd reap the benefits of.

No.

Cora was enthusiastic about the task at hand.

She started moving her hips as she kept her hands on my chest. There was a seductive look in her eyes. Seeing it caught me off guard. Up until this point, I hadn't expected Cora would have been like this in the bedroom. Coming to the realization that she could take charge of a situation in her line of work and when we were being intimate was a huge turn-on.

My hands roamed over Cora's beautiful body as she worked the both of us up. I did my best to allow her to lead us. And she did an amazing job.

When I had my mouth between her legs, I found myself not only focused on that task but also imagining what this was going to be like with her.

While I had imagined it much differently, suffice it to say I was not the least bit disappointed by how this was turning out.

Cora's hands flew to the headboard as one of mine went to her ass and the other to her breast. I lifted my head slightly and closed my mouth over her nipple on the opposite side. The second I did that, I not only heard

Cora's moan but also felt the spasm between her legs as she tightened around and clenched my shaft tighter. I couldn't stop myself from groaning, and Cora arched her back, shoving her breast deeper into my mouth.

Clamping one arm tight around her waist, I planted my feet into the bed and began to thrust hard into her.

"Ben," she cried out.

My tongue flicked faster over her nipple as I increased the pace of my thrusts. I knew she had wanted to stay in control, but I couldn't give it all to her. My instincts wouldn't let me.

Cora pushed back from the headboard, moving only as much as she could with me having such a firm grip on her, and lowered her mouth to mine.

Her tongue swept into my mouth for a few strokes, but she ultimately disconnected and warned, "I'm going to come."

"Give it to me, Cora," I urged her.

She didn't hesitate. Because in the next moment, I watched as the control she had been holding onto slipped, and her orgasm took over. The sight of her like that undid me, and it wasn't more than another few thrusts before I joined her.

Cora and I were tangled up in my bed. We'd been wrapped in each other's arms for a long time. Neither one of us had spoken since I'd returned from the bathroom.

But it wasn't awkward.

It just felt good.

Comfortable.

And it was something I'd never really cared to do with a woman before now.

As I ran my fingers through her hair, I declared, "I want to take you to my place next weekend."

Cora lifted her cheek from my chest to look at me. "Um, we're in your place now," she said, clearly confused by my statement.

"Not this place," I started. "My home in Rosewood. I want to take you there next weekend. We'll leave Friday night, spend the whole weekend, and come back to the city early Monday morning."

Disappointment washed over her. "I can't."

"What? Why not?"

"The last wedding I have scheduled for this year is next weekend," she explained. "I won't be able to go with you out to your place. But I would definitely love to see it sometime."

I'd forgotten about the wedding. Now I understood Cora's disappointment. Before I had the chance to respond, she suggested, "Maybe we can get together during the week, though. I'm sure you're busy with work, but if you can squeeze in a lunch date one day, we could at least see each other."

"Alright, we'll do that," I agreed. "Since you showed up at my office this week, I'll come to your office one day next week."

"That works for me," she said, beaming up at me.

"Though, since my apartment isn't far from my office, we could also meet there."

I cocked an eyebrow. "You're a feisty girl."

Without missing a beat, Cora shot back, "So are you suggesting that you'd rather wait two weeks before we can do this a second time?"

"No. But a big part of that is because we'll be doing it a second time in about five minutes," I promised her.

I felt her hips press into my side and gave her a smirk.

"Can you just make sure to call my office and let Abigail know what day works best for you so she can put it in my calendar?" I asked. "I don't think I have any meetings next week that will interfere, so any day that's good for you should work for me."

Cora nodded and asked, "What about the following week, too? Can we do one day then as well?"

I grinned. "Only if you promise to come with me out to my place in Rosewood that weekend."

With a sense of determination I'd seen in her several times before now, she challenged, "Try and stop me."

All I could do was laugh. The more I saw this side of her, the more I liked it.

When I took in Cora's eyes again, I noticed she seemed a bit despondent. "Is everything okay?" I wondered.

She sighed. "I'm just a little disappointed I have to wait another five minutes for you to be the boss."

My arm tightened around her briefly before I rolled her to her back. After I kissed her, I declared, "Work starts early today."

"Fine," she said against my lips. "But just because I'm starting early doesn't mean I'm planning to leave early."

"That's good because I think we're going to have to pull an all-nighter tonight."

Cora's response was to part her thighs, run her fingers through my hair, and lift her head to touch her mouth to mine. That was the only time she took charge because from that point forward, I was the boss.

CHAPTER 10

Cora

I WAS SEATED AT A BOOTH BY THE WINDOW WAITING FOR BEN to meet me. It was Thursday, the week after Julia's wedding, and Ben and I were going to be having our second lunch date. I knew we were going to be spending the weekend together, but I just couldn't wait another day to see him.

Things with Ben had gotten serious over the last two weeks.

Admittedly, they'd gotten serious very quickly considering we'd only met just over a month ago. I had no regrets, though.

The day I met him at his office and ended up back at his place in the city, I hadn't had any intentions of taking things that far with him. But he was willing to talk with me about my issues concerning what was developing between us and address them. Not only that, but he also said what I needed to hear to know that we were both on the same page.

Ben never once tried to deny the truth. He knew that

he had a reputation and understood that I had valid concerns. Sure, according to him, I was the first woman he had been with since realizing he wanted more out of his romantic life. I believed him when he explained it. And I never once thought that just because he hadn't had any serious relationships before me that he didn't deserve to ever have one if that's what he wanted in his life.

So, when he shared why it was me that he'd been interested in pursuing something serious with, I couldn't stop myself from going after more.

And ever since then, he hadn't made me regret it.

We spent the rest of that weekend together, enjoying each other. When Monday rolled around, it was back to work for both of us. As Ben told me I should, I checked my schedule and called his secretary to set up our lunch dates.

On Wednesday afternoon, I left my office a little early and went back to my apartment. Ten minutes after I arrived, Ben showed up and brought sandwiches from a local deli with him. Eating was an afterthought, though. It had been a few days since we'd seen each other, so we both had other things on our mind.

Following our afternoon romp, we ate.

And over lunch, I learned a little bit more about the man I knew I was falling for.

"You know," I started after swallowing a bite of my sandwich. "I've been wanting to ask you about something ever since we talked last Friday."

"Okay. What did you want to know?"

"You mentioned that you thought you had everything

you wanted in life. Of those things were your family and friends. Can you tell me about them? Do they live here?" I asked.

"Most of them live in New York, but not in Manhattan," he began. "My parents are still living in the house they raised my brother and me in."

My eyes widened in surprise. "You have a brother?"

Ben nodded.

"And he's not in the same business as you?"

He shook his head. "Will wanted to travel the world. He met a girl years ago who wanted to take that journey with him. Now, the two of them are married, run a wildly successful travel blog, and have visited close to seventy-five different countries."

"So, you don't see him very often?"

Ben let out a laugh. "I see him more than you'd think. It's just not in person. We video chat almost weekly, and he comes home for Christmas every year. Even still, it sucks not having him around."

That made me happy to hear. Not the fact that he didn't have his brother around. I just liked knowing that Ben had a close relationship with his brother.

"Who's older?"

"I'm thirty-five; Will is thirty-two."

"And where is he now?" I wondered.

"Nepal."

"Wow, that's incredible," I marveled.

"What about you?" Ben asked. "Do you have any siblings?"

Shaking my head, I answered, "No. I'm an only child.

But Kenzie and I have known each other since we were in second grade. I'm guessing we're as close to sisters as it gets."

"And your parents?" he pressed for more. "Are they in New York?"

I smiled at him. "Yes, but Manhattan is not their thing. They're mostly homebodies, but if they travel, they'll head up to the Finger Lakes."

Ben was just about to say something when my phone rang. I hated having the interruption during our time together. Glancing down at my phone, I saw Julia was calling.

"I'm sorry," I lamented. "It's my bride for this weekend's wedding."

"Answer it," he ordered. "It's okay."

I tapped on the screen and held the phone to my ear. I barely managed to greet Julia when she shrieked in my ear, "We have a major disaster!"

It was so unlike her to be yelling that I immediately grew alert. Ben noticed and eyed me curiously.

"What's wrong?" I asked.

"My fiancé's family is the problem!" she spat. "Apparently, there was a disagreement between a group of cousins or aunts recently. I don't know. I'm not even sure I've met all of them, considering the size of his extended family. Anyway, we've gotten a couple phone calls from members of the family requesting that they aren't seated next to certain other individuals. The seating chart is a nightmare now. I don't know what to do."

This was not a big deal. I mean, I'm sure to Julia it seemed like the end of the world, but this was nothing.

"Okay, first, calm down and take a few deep breaths."

Once I gave her some time to do that, I asked, "Now, where are you?"

"Home."

"Can you meet me at my office in fifteen minutes with your seating chart and all of your last-minute seat requests?"

There was a beat of silence before she surmised, "I'll probably be closer to twenty or twenty-five minutes."

"That's no problem," I assured her. "I'll meet you there then, and we'll have this sorted out in no time. I promise."

I heard her take in a deep breath. "Okay. Thank you so much, Cora."

"You're welcome."

I disconnected the call and looked up at Ben. "Is your family crazy?" I wondered.

He shook his head and let out a laugh. "For the most part, they're pretty mellow."

I smiled in response.

"You have to head back to your office now?" he wondered.

"She needs a little extra time to get there, so I'd say we've got a solid ten minutes."

Ben brought his hand up to cup my cheek. His thumb stroked over the skin there before he stated, "I have an idea how we can spend those ten minutes."

Without any hesitation, I demanded, "Kiss me."

So, he did.

And when we parted ways that afternoon, we made

plans to touch base here and there until our next lunch date. We'd managed to do that. Sometimes, it was just a quick text to let the other know that they were on our mind. Other times, it was a phone call when we were able to catch up a bit more.

Now, thankfully, the day had arrived for our second lunch date, and I couldn't wait to see him again.

The memories of the last two weeks had gone through my mind when I suddenly realized I'd been sitting for a long while waiting for Ben. I pulled out my phone to check the time and to see if I missed a call or a text from him. Looking at it, I confirmed that not only was he fifteen minutes late, but he also hadn't reached out to tell me that he was running behind. Ben was always punctual. And if he had any reason to believe that he might get tied up, he made the effort to communicate that.

I began worrying that something had happened to him, so I figured it was best to call and check that he was okay. By the time I'd gotten to my list of contacts and was about to tap on his name, something caught the corner of my eye.

Turning my head to the side, I took it in. Like a bad accident, I couldn't peel my eyes away from the scene in front of me. Across the street, not even fifty feet in the opposite direction was Ben's flashy car. I knew it was his because it wasn't every day you saw one of them driving around the city. Not only that, but the fact that Ben had exited the car on the driver's side and moved around to the passenger side was enough of an indication.

But what happened next made me sick.

He opened the door, and a woman stepped out.

Lisa.

I didn't want to jump to conclusions, but I couldn't help it. What else was I to think? I knew that she was a client, but did he really take his clients to lunch *in his car?*

Why wouldn't they meet for lunch?

And why was he even at lunch with her when he was supposed to be with me?

Watching him walk beside her into the restaurant, I wanted to turn my attention elsewhere. But I couldn't. My eyes were glued to them.

Something deep in the back of my mind was gnawing away at me telling me to give him the benefit of the doubt, but my heart couldn't. It hurt too bad.

The moment Ben and Lisa stepped inside the restaurant, I got the attention of my waitress. I didn't know what look was on my face, but she must have seen something that wasn't good. "Is everything alright?" she asked.

"Yeah, um, I just, I need the check for my drink," I said.

She grew concerned and pointed out, "But you haven't had anything to eat yet."

I nodded. "I'm just not feeling well. I need to get out of here please," I told her.

"Sure."

She took off to get my check. I pulled some cash out of my purse so the minute the waitress returned with the bill, I threw a twenty-dollar bill at her and told her to keep the change.

Then, I dashed out the door.

I should have turned in the opposite direction. I should have cut my losses and walked away.

Apparently, though, I was a glutton for punishment. Because I crossed the street and moved toward the restaurant. I didn't know if I was going to go in. I didn't know what I would say if I did. Something was pulling me in that direction, forcing me there.

Just before the restaurant, my stride slowed until I eventually stopped a few feet from it. I didn't need to move any farther. I could see them at their table through the window. They weren't right at the window, but still in plain sight. Neither one of them could see me since their backs were to me.

But I could see them.

I could see that Ben had scooted his chair around the table closer to her, just like he'd done with me that time in the café. That time he'd managed to make me believe he was worth taking a chance on.

And standing there, on the New York City sidewalk, I realized something. Either I was a naïve fool or Ben was just really good. I ultimately decided it had to be a bit of both. Because with his arm around her back and her head resting in the crook of his shoulder, a tear fell from each eye and down my cheeks.

I was crying because I'd all too quickly forgotten how men like Ben worked. He was so smooth; it was hard to resist him.

Even a woman who was married couldn't resist him. I watched as she tipped her head back and reached her hand up to cup the side of his face. I couldn't read the look in his eyes, and that made me feel sick.

No longer able to stand it, I took off running down the street before I had to see what I knew was going to come next. I continued to run until I made it to Kenzie's apartment. And I waited there, sitting on the floor outside her door until she got home from work three hours later.

Kenzie took one look at me and whispered something under her breath. Then, she slipped her key in the door and gently instructed, "Come inside."

"I'm so sorry, Cora," Kenzie lamented from the opposite side of the couch.

I'd just shared everything that had happened with her. And she was doing what any good best friend would do. She gave me an alcoholic drink and dried my tears.

I'd gotten the tears out and was now sitting there, staring off into space, slowly shaking my head back and forth in disbelief and disappointment. "I was so foolish, Kenz. So incredibly foolish."

"You weren't," she insisted.

Turning my attention to her, I shared, "I allowed myself to be swept off my feet by him, even when I already knew something like this would happen."

"But he was convincing," she started. "With everything you told me, Cora, anyone would have believed him. And there's nothing wrong with you for wanting to give someone the benefit of the doubt. For wanting to believe he was being honest."

That was the understatement of the century because it was precisely what I'd been thinking about as I sat waiting for him in that restaurant.

"I should have stuck to my guns," I concluded. "I never should have fallen for his lies. It was a bad move on my part. I knew it. I knew this would happen."

Kenzie pleaded, "Cora, don't let this guy do this to you. This was all on him. There is no reason for you to beat yourself up about the fact that you liked a guy who was handsome, charming, and attentive. He ticks all the right boxes."

I continued to shake my head, so disappointed with myself. "But after what I went through with Josh, I knew Ben was not a smart move."

"That's bullshit. Just because Josh was an asshole, doesn't mean you don't deserve to find someone who will treat you right."

My friend. I loved her. "I'm not saying that, Kenz. I'm just saying that experience tells me how guys like Josh and Ben are. They're good at what they do. They know how to play the part of the devoted and loyal boyfriend. They'll easily have you eating out of the palm of their hand. They're ruthless and driven businessmen. They know how to get what they want. And just when you feel yourself succumbing to it, they show you who they really are. My mistake in all of this was thinking that I could ever be enough for someone like Ben."

I heard myself say the words, but I didn't like the way they sounded. Not only because I thought I should have been enough for Ben, but also because he had truly made me feel that way up until I saw what I did today. Every word he ever said to me had felt so real, and I wondered how I could have gotten it so wrong.

Just then, a chime came from inside my purse, indicating I'd received a text. My eyes went back to Kenzie. The moment they did, a second text came in. We waited, neither of us moving, but nothing else came after that.

"Face the music?" she eventually asked, holding out my purse to me.

I took it from her, dug out my phone, and lit up the display. Two texts from Ben.

Hey baby, hope you had a good day.

That was followed by the one that sent a knife through my heart.

Can't wait to see you tomorrow.

"Ben?" she asked.

I gave her a nod.

"What did he say?"

There was no way I could repeat the words, so I turned the phone around and held it out to her. She read the texts, looked at me, and wondered, "What are you going to say?"

I glanced down at the display again.

Can't wait to see you tomorrow.

All I could think was: *What the hell happened to today?*

Of course, I didn't type that. I did what any

self-respecting city girl would do. I held down the power button on my phone and turned it off.

Then, I spent the night at my best friend's apartment. And when I tried to fall asleep that night, all I could think was I hated myself for missing the guy who'd done what Ben did.

CHAPTER 11

Cora

I WAS WOKEN BY THE SOUND OF THE BEDROOM DOOR OPENING. My eyes fluttered open, and the second I saw Kenzie, it all came flooding back.

"You look like you didn't sleep," she pointed out as she came toward the bed with a cup of coffee in each of her hands.

I took one of the mugs from her and confessed, "I tossed and turned all night."

"Did you hear from him again?" she wondered as she sat down on the bed.

"I don't know. I never turned my phone back on," I told her.

Kenzie took in a deep breath and something about the way she did it told me she had news to share.

"What is it?" I asked.

She sighed. "I wanted to give him the benefit of the doubt. I didn't say anything yesterday because you were far too raw, and I needed to just be here to listen to you. I know you probably aren't feeling much better today, but truthfully, I was really hoping that maybe you misinterpreted what you saw."

That didn't upset me. Kenzie was a hopeless romantic. In the end, she always wanted to see the girl get the guy. I could tell from the way she was looking at me, despite all her hoping and dreaming that this story would be one with a happy ending, that she had the very harsh truth smack her in the face. I just didn't know what it was that enlightened her.

"Tell me," I begged, knowing there was something.

It was then I noticed she'd entered the room with not only the two coffee mugs in her hands but also her iPad tucked under her arm. She set her coffee mug down and opened her tablet. When she handed it over, I understood the look on her face.

Trouble in Paradise?

That was the headline.

And the subtitle read: **Seen out with another woman, Ben Mason proves he's not a one-woman kind of guy. And check out how his former flame handled the news.**

Oh God.

This was already mortifying.

Front and center was a picture of Ben and Lisa as they entered the restaurant. They were both oblivious to the cameras.

I knew I shouldn't have done it to myself, but I couldn't help it. I started reading the article.

With reports of a divorce announcement swirling, online dating site founder, Lisa Ross, was seen cozying up with billionaire hedge-fund manager, Ben Mason, at a restaurant on Thursday afternoon. Mason held Ross in his arms, and the pair barely managed to separate themselves long enough to eat their meal.

The text ended there as several pictures of the two inside the restaurant came up as I continued to scroll.

All I could think as I looked at each one of them was that she was getting a divorce. She was a multi-millionaire who founded a matchmaking or dating site and was divorcing her husband, and now she was in the arms of the man I loved.

Yep.

Ben was the man I loved.

After only a little over a month, I had fallen in love with a liar.

My mind went blank as I stared at the pictures and scrolled until I had no choice but to stop. I was staring at a picture of me. In it, I was looking devastated as I stared into the window of the restaurant with tears rolling down my cheeks.

Just beneath the photo, there was additional text.

While Mason seems to have moved on, it's clear that his former lover has not. Cora Daniels watched from afar as the new couple flaunted their affections for one another. Moments later, Daniels was photographed running down the street.

Sure enough, beneath the text, I found several more photos of me running away. Under them, more text.

An hour after they arrived, Mason and Ross were seen leaving the restaurant in his McLaren, both seemingly unaware that Daniels had ever seen them.

Following that line of text were two more pictures: one of Ben and Lisa walking out of the restaurant and the other of him pulling away from the curb in his car with her sitting beside him.

I dropped the iPad, looked at Kenzie, and grumbled, "When did they learn my name? Honestly, couldn't I have just remained a mystery?"

"I hear you. It's awful," she agreed. "What are you going to do?"

Shaking my head, still feeling an overwhelming level of disappointment in myself, I admitted, "Nothing. What can I do?"

Kenzie returned a look that told me she completely understood my predicament. "Are you going to hang out here today?" she asked.

"What time is it?"

"Almost seven-thirty," she told me. "I know it's early, but I didn't want to leave without making sure you were okay."

"I might stay for another hour or two if that's alright with you. No matter how much I might want to stay here indefinitely, I can't sit around sulking forever. I just need a little bit to pull myself together this morning."

"I hate to leave you, but I've got to get to work," she stated. "If you need me at all, just give me a call. I'll set my spare key out on the kitchen counter so you can lock up when you leave."

"Thanks, Kenz."

Kenzie scooted toward me, wrapped her arms

around me, and squeezed. "You'll get through this, Cora. I promise."

I knew she was right because I was who I was. Ben might have made a fool of me, but those tears he got from me in that photo were all he'd have as evidence that I felt something for him. I made a vow right there that by the time I left Kenzie's apartment this morning, I would not allow myself to shed another tear over Ben.

Ben

My phone rang.

It was just after eight-thirty Friday morning, and I was at my place. I'd already been up for several hours working. Earlier in the week, I had decided to work a few late nights so that I could spend most of my day today with Cora.

I figured I'd wake up before five, check the international markets, make sure nothing concerning was happening, and get in a workout. I'd managed to do that, take a shower, make myself some food, and get some more work done.

I had no plans to go into the office today because after I met Cora for our lunch date this afternoon, I was hoping I'd be able to convince her to take the rest of her day off from work. I wanted us to head out of the city and into Rosewood as soon as we could.

Over the last few days, we'd only managed to talk a few times. Last night, I sent a text to her, but never heard back. It was unlike her not to respond, but to be fair, I'd reached out rather late as well. I figured she probably went to bed early.

I also assumed that she was the reason my phone was ringing now.

Unfortunately, it wasn't her. Looking at the display, I saw my brother's name. I connected the call, and greeted him, "Shouldn't you be at dinner now? What time is it there?"

Will let out a laugh and answered, "It's about quarter after six here. And yes, we should be at dinner. But when I was getting ready to go out, Ashley was busy getting sidetracked doing research."

That wasn't surprising. "She was scoping out your next few locations?" I guessed, knowing that my sister-in-law was always planning their next adventure.

Will grunted. "Not at all. She was trying to figure out what's going on with you," he informed me.

"Me? What are you talking about?" I asked.

"You know Ash is addicted to those gossip websites. She gets on, and I swear, sometimes she could stay there for hours reading nonsense. Anyway, after we talked to you two weeks ago and you shared about the new woman you've been seeing, Ash has been all over that. She scoured the internet looking for photos of the two of you together. And I'm telling you now, you're lucky I managed to get her in the shower so she could start getting ready. Because if she knew I was on the phone with you right now, I'd not be eating dinner anytime soon."

Will was talking in circles. I had no idea what was going on. "What is Ash's issue?" I asked.

"She's pissed at you."

That made no sense. "Why?" I wondered.

"Because for the last two weeks all she's talked about is how she's so happy you seem to be settling down. She's seen the pictures of you and Cora and was really hoping to meet her when we come back home for Christmas. But for the last three hours, she's been on a rampage because it seems you're still into breaking hearts."

I remained silent because I still had no clue what Will was talking about.

Ignoring my silence, my brother pressed, "What happened? I thought you really liked this one. You said she was different… special."

"She is," I insisted.

There was hesitation on his end before he questioned, "Well, then why the hell did you have another woman in your arms yesterday afternoon while the woman you claim you have real feelings for watched and cried?"

For a brief moment, I figured he must have misunderstood whatever it was Ash had told him. But what worried me was that he said Cora had been crying.

"Can I ask where this is coming from?"

Will rattled off the name of the website. I pulled it up on my laptop and saw that I was their top storyline for the day.

I was used to this. The photos and the reporters making assumptions about my personal life. I never really paid much attention to it, but I also never had anyone in my life who could be affected by the things that were reported either.

As I scrolled through and read what had been written, I started feeling worse and worse because they painted a pretty ugly picture. Even still, I tried to remain calm. Cora had seen Lisa before. She knew Lisa was a client, and I told her that was all it was between us. But it wasn't until I approached the end of the article and saw it that a cold empty pit settled in my stomach.

Cora.

My beautiful Cora was standing there outside of the restaurant, visibly upset, watching me hold another woman in my arms. It didn't matter that it was all misconstrued and that everything reported wasn't true. All that mattered was that she saw that, believed it was something that it wasn't, and she never texted me back last night.

"Fuck," I muttered.

"False report?" Will asked.

"Of course it is," I retorted, continuing to scroll and seeing Cora run down the street. "What the hell am I going to do?"

"Why were you even out with Lisa Ross?" he chastised me. He didn't give me a moment to respond before he went on, "And fair warning, Ash does not like her. She said if you bring her to Mom and Dad's for Christmas, she's boycotting."

I could feel the anger building inside me. "I'm not bringing Lisa anywhere. She's one of my clients. And what they posted here is not what they're making it look like it is, even if the woman did try hitting on me."

"Well, then it looks like you're going to have a lot of explaining and groveling to do because the woman we saw in those pictures, the woman you claim means something to you, was broken."

I couldn't believe this. For the better part of the day yesterday and all night long, Cora had been under the impression that I was cheating on her.

Never.

I would never do that to her.

I had to explain it to her.

I only hoped she would let me.

"She never responded to my texts last night," I told my brother.

"Can you blame her?" he retorted.

I couldn't. Well, part of me couldn't. But Cora knew. She had to know how I felt about her. Why didn't she just come in and talk to me? I could have introduced her and explained it right there. She would have saved herself the heartache. She would have saved me from my current torment and fear that she might not ever speak to me again.

"She has to know how I feel about her, Will. She should have known I'd never do that to her," I asserted.

"How do you feel about her?" he questioned me.

I took in a deep breath. Could I say it? In my mind, I knew. I loved her. More than I could have ever imagined. And now I might not ever get the chance to tell her. Because I had no doubt she wasn't going to want to listen to a thing I said. Not after everything she'd been through with her ex. In her mind, I was no better than him.

"Your silence tells me how you feel about her, Ben. I think that you're going to have to find a way to tell her because it's obvious she doesn't know."

"Is she going to give me the chance?" I asked, knowing he didn't have the answer.

Will let out a little laugh and said, "I know I'm living almost ten hours in the future, but I don't have access to that kind of information. You're just going to have to hope for the best."

"Fuck," I swore.

"I'll let you go so you can get to work on that," he started. "With any luck, Ash and I can meet her at Christmas."

"I fucking hope so."

Will and I disconnected, and I took another look at Cora's sad face on my screen. Lifting my finger up to touch her face on the monitor, I whispered, "Baby."

Snapping myself out of it, I pulled her name up on my phone and tapped on the screen. It didn't even ring and went straight to voicemail.

"Hey, it's Cora. Leave me a message."

"Cora, it's me," I started. "It's not what you think. It's not what they're making it out to be. Please… please call me back. I want to explain."

I disconnected, threw my phone down on the desk, and walked to my bedroom. After changing my clothes, I locked up and left. Sitting around and waiting for a call that might not ever come, I had to go out.

Since it was on the way to her place and I found parking, I stopped at Cora's office first. Part of me was surprised that she wasn't at work, but based on what I knew she thought happened, I should have expected it.

It would have taken me longer to drive to Cora's apartment than it would to walk, so I went on foot. When I got to her building, I pushed the bell to be buzzed up, but she never answered it. I pulled out my phone and tried calling her again.

Nothing.

I wondered if she might have been at her friend's place, but I didn't even know what Kenzie's last name was so that I could try to locate her.

It dawned on me that Cora and I were supposed to have lunch today, but I doubted she'd show up. Even still, if I hadn't been able to get in touch with her before then, I'd go and wait for her.

Just then, someone walked out of Cora's building. I held the door open for the woman and went inside after she walked through. After making my way up to Cora's floor, I knocked on her door. "Cora!" I called.

She never answered.

I went to my recent calls list, tapped on Cora's name, and got her voicemail again. As I prepared to leave another message, I paced the hallway outside her apartment.

"Cora, baby, please call me," I begged. My voice no longer sounded like my own. It was filled with desperation and despair. I could barely get the words out past the lump in my throat. "I know what you must be thinking, but it's not true. I promise. Cora, I promise it's not true. Just please call me so I can explain."

I pulled the phone from my ear, disconnected, and dropped my gaze to the ground. After taking a few breaths to settle myself, I turned to leave. When I did, I took only one step before I stopped in my tracks.

There she was.

Standing right in front of me.

And I couldn't read a single thing in the expression on her face.

"Cora—" I got out before she cut me off.

"You should go," she deadpanned.

I shook my head. "I can't. Not without talking to you first."

Cora walked to her door, slipped her key inside, and opened it. I felt the slightest bit of relief that she was at least willing to hear me out.

Only, no sooner did she step into her apartment when she turned around and spoke with such a firm and final tone. "Goodbye, Ben."

Then, she closed the door in my face.

CHAPTER 12

Cora

A RUSH OF AIR LEFT MY LUNGS AS I LEANED MY BACK AGAINST the door. I couldn't handle him being here.

"Cora?" he called through the door as he gently knocked.

I closed my eyes.

"Please, baby. Let me in."

I did that already, and you trashed it, I thought.

I had to keep reminding myself of that because when I got off the elevator and walked down the hall, I was not prepared for what hearing him leave that message would do to me. It was his voice. The agony and anguish in his voice as he left me a message was more than I could bear. I didn't understand how I could want to hug him to comfort him and strangle him for hurting me all at the same time.

Maybe it was unfair of me not to at least allow him the opportunity to speak. Maybe that was childish. But I knew Ben. More importantly, I knew myself. And I had no doubt that he'd say all the right things, and I'd believe him. I'd do that because that's how badly I wanted him to be that guy for me.

The good we had between us was that good. There was so much more left to explore with him, and I wanted that.

So, I couldn't allow him the opportunity to talk to me. I wasn't strong enough just yet to hear what he had to say.

I stood at my door for another ten minutes. Ben stopped knocking. He didn't call my name again. Stepping away from the door, I let out a sigh of relief that he'd finally gone.

Then, I tried my best to get back to some semblance of normal. Going to the office was completely out of the question for me today, but I could pretend like I was having a long weekend.

I moved to the bathroom and took a shower. In it, I broke my vow to myself. Because I lasted about three minutes before I heard his tortured voice in my head. That's when I broke down, sobbing, as the water ran over me. When I finally got through that fit, I picked myself up off the floor of my bathtub and finished my shower. Afterward, I took my time and pampered myself a bit as I got ready.

Nearly three hours after I walked past Ben and into my apartment, I heard a commotion in the hall outside my door. I moved closer to it and listened.

"You can't just be here," I heard a woman say.

I was shocked to hear Ben's voice reply, "I'm not leaving."

"You don't have a key to any apartment in this building, and you obviously don't have anyone here that you're friends with. You can't just loiter in the hall; it's unsafe. I'll have to call the cops if you don't leave," the woman insisted.

I gasped.

"Then call the cops," Ben dared her.

My eyes widened.

Without thinking, I opened my door. Ben's devastated eyes came to mine. I took a step out into the hall, saw the woman who'd been threatening to call the cops on Ben, and assured her, "It's okay, ma'am. There's no need to call the police. I know him."

"He shouldn't be sitting outside your door in the hallway of an apartment building where other people live. It's not safe," she scolded me.

"You're right. I'm sorry."

At that, she turned and ambled off.

Standing in my doorway, I turned my attention to Ben. "Why did you come back here?" I asked.

"I never left, Cora."

My eyes widened again. "You've been sitting out here for the last three hours?"

He gave me a quick nod.

"Why? Ben, you need to go," I insisted.

"There are only two ways I'm leaving here. Either with you or in handcuffs."

He couldn't be serious.

I sighed. "I'm not going with you."

"You made plans to have lunch with me today," he declared. "I'm not letting you back out of that."

Suddenly, I was angry. "Excuse me? First of all, *you* don't *let* me do anything. I'll do whatever I want. Second, and just as important to note, our plans for lunch were *yesterday*. You know, when you stood me up so you could go out with another woman."

Ben's eyes narrowed. "Our plans were for today. It's on my calendar. That's what you set up with Abigail."

I gave him a look that told him I didn't care what excuse he came up with. "No, Ben. I told Abigail Thursday. The point was to be able to see you before the end of the week. I mean, we were supposed to be seeing each other after work today and heading out of the city. What sense would it have made for me to want to see you at lunch only to have to have you go back to work for a few hours before we could go to Rosewood? I scheduled for Thursday."

Ben hesitated a moment, thinking. "She's new," he finally declared.

"Obviously," I scoffed. "Lisa's fresh meat on the market with her impending divorce and all. It's no surprise Ben Mason would want a piece of that."

"I'm talking about Abigail," Ben replied through gritted teeth. "She's new. My old receptionist had her last day two weeks ago. Abby is still learning the ropes. Apparently, she put you in the calendar on the wrong day."

Okay, so that explanation made sense. Especially when I thought back to the day I had first gone to Ben's office. I remembered seeing the older woman there going over things with the younger woman. That older woman must have been his former receptionist, and she must have been training the new one.

But that didn't matter. It still didn't change anything. He was out with another woman, and it was entirely too friendly for it to be a business meeting. I wasn't going to buy the explanation that he was simply out with a client.

Before I could share this with him, he snapped, "And that bit about Lisa and me was uncalled for. I'm not going to stand here and listen to you say things that you know aren't true. Lisa is a business client. You know that. We discussed this weeks ago."

I blinked in surprise at his reaction. "Are you… are you *angry* at me??" I countered.

"You're damn right I am," he clipped.

"You want me to believe that Lisa's just your client?" I scoffed. "Let me ask you this, Benjamin. How many of your other clients end up with your chair pulled close to theirs so you can wrap them in your arms? How many of them get to rest their heads in the crook of your shoulder? Huh? Can you tell me that?"

"None," he deadpanned.

My point being made, I stepped back into my apartment and started to close the door when Ben spoke again. "But none of my other clients got news hours before a meeting with me that their mother who lives out of state was just diagnosed with terminal cancer either."

I completely froze.

Ben and I stared at each other in silence for several long, agonizing moments.

Finally, he broke the silence. "I didn't even know

until she blurted it out at the restaurant. We were there to discuss her plans moving forward because of the divorce. I swear that to you. And I know what you saw yesterday, Cora. I understand how it must have felt for you to see that, especially after what your ex did to you. But I'm not him. I never lied to you, and I have zero romantic interest in Lisa. You have to believe me, baby."

The stinging in my nose and the burning in my throat prevented me from responding. At that moment, I had so many emotions running through me, and I couldn't begin to process any of them.

Thankfully, I didn't have to because Ben continued, "I had no idea that anything was wrong yesterday. If I had, I would have been here sooner. I only found out about it this morning when my brother called me from Nepal. And Cora, when I saw those pictures of you this morning..." He trailed off. After a moment, he went on, "I hated seeing your tears. I am so sorry you got hurt, and I'll do anything to make this right."

"How do I know you're not making this all up?" I asked. "Maybe you just know how to play the part of the worried and wounded man to get what you want. How do I know that you mean what you're saying and it's not just you being a really good actor?"   .

He shrugged. "I guess you don't, which makes me wonder what you think everything before this was between us. Either you believe me and trust that I've been honest with you from the beginning and will continue to be honest with you, or you don't. And if you don't, no matter how much I love you, this will never work."

My breath caught in my lungs. I stared up at Ben with wide, curious eyes.

He loved me?

"You love me?" I whispered.

"Do you think I would have waited out here on the floor for three hours if I didn't?" he countered.

My chin began quivering as tears welled up in my eyes. Ben took two steps toward me, caught my chin between his thumb and forefinger, and pleaded, "Come with me to Rosewood."

I couldn't. That touch on his face would haunt me forever. I'd always be wondering.

Ben must have realized I was struggling to agree to his request because his face twisted with a reaction I couldn't quite read.

"What's wrong?" I asked.

"I have to tell you something," he replied cautiously. After a brief pause he added, "About something that happened at my lunch with Lisa yesterday."

My body instantly tensed. He kissed her. I knew it. I knew he kissed her. Right after I took off running down the street.

"What is it?" I asked, even though I already knew.

Ben looked devastated. Even still, he pressed on. "Everything I told you about what happened was true. But there was something else."

I swallowed hard and waited for it.

"She tried to kiss me," he said.

Tried?

"Tried?" I asked, trying to keep my voice neutral.

Ben dipped his chin. "You were right, baby. She was interested in me. I was there thinking I was comforting a woman who'd just received horrible news. And I was. Her mother is terminal. But Lisa also took advantage of the situation. While I was there trying to be a nice guy by offering her comfort, she reached up and touched my face. I was so caught off guard by it that I froze. But I managed to pull myself together only seconds before she was able to kiss me. As soon as I realized what she was doing, I immediately pulled away. I didn't want to be a dick because she'd just gotten the news about her mom, but I also made it clear to her that I wasn't interested."

I closed my eyes and let out the breath I'd been holding.

Before I could respond, I felt Ben's hand at the side of my neck. His thumb stroked over the skin at the front of my throat. When I opened my eyes, he lamented, "I'm so sorry, baby."

It seemed as though I had a choice to make. And Ben was right. Either I believed him and wanted this to work, or I didn't trust him and we'd never work. It wouldn't be fair to me to be with someone I had to constantly second guess, and it wouldn't be fair to him if I was constantly questioning his loyalty.

Despite what I saw yesterday, everything else about Ben had felt so real. He was attentive. He cared. He asked me about my day, and whenever he was around, I always felt happier. I didn't want things to end between us. And he'd just shared the worst of what happened yesterday without me having to ask him about it.

"Can we go to Rosewood now?" I asked.

Relief swept through him. Ben immediately slipped his arms around my waist, lifted me up, and carried me back inside my apartment. Then, he buried his face in my neck as he kicked the door shut with his foot.

"I promise it's all good now, Kenz."

"You'll give me the details on Monday when you're back?" she asked.

"Yes. You'll be the first call I make when I'm back in the office," I assured her. "But just so you know, you were right this morning. I misinterpreted things."

"Alright. But if you need anything before then, you know you've got me," she reminded me.

I did. It was something I was always grateful for. I knew she'd be there for me whenever I needed her. "I know. Thank you for everything, Kenzie."

"You're welcome, Cora. Love you."

"Love you, too."

I disconnected with my best friend before I walked outside to join Ben on his deck. We were at his home in Rosewood. When we arrived a few hours ago, he gave me the grand tour. It was a gorgeous farmhouse on a huge piece of land. It was the complete opposite of what I would have expected him to own.

As I walked over to where Ben was sitting with his feet up and the fire pit going, he asked, "Did you update your friend?"

I nodded and sat down next to him. Ben immediately wrapped one arm around my shoulders, the other across my knees, and tugged me toward him before covering me with a blanket. Once my cheek was pressed to his chest and my legs draped over his thighs, I answered, "Yeah. I didn't give her details now, but I wanted her to know that you and I are good. She was good to me last night, and I know she was worried about me today, so I had to give her something."

Ben squeezed me in response.

"So, you never told me how your brother found out about what was going on before you did," I remarked, suddenly curious about how it had all gone down.

He let out a laugh and stated, "Will's wife, Ashley. She is a celebrity news gossip fiend. I don't consider myself a celebrity, but she knows I end up in the tabloids. When I talked to Will a couple weeks ago and told him and Ash about you, they knew I was serious about you. Ash has been waiting for this time to come, so she started scouring the internet for anything she could find on you. Ultimately, she kept tabs on us and saw an article."

I smiled and shared, "She sounds like Kenzie. You would think my best friend got paid to read the tabloids."

"I'm just grateful you decided to give this another chance," he said. "According to Will, Ash was planning to boycott Christmas."

I tipped my head back and looked up at him. "Really?"

Ben nodded. "Yeah. I guess from the little bit that she'd found out on you, she decided she liked you and couldn't wait to meet you. As it is, Will had to call me in secret when Ash was getting ready for dinner. Had she known he was calling me, she would've let me have it."

"I already like this girl," I decided.

Ben kissed my forehead and squeezed my thigh.

The two of us sat there a long time, neither of us saying a word. I took the time to just enjoy being back in his arms.

"It's beautiful here," I said softly.

"You like it?" he asked.

"Yes, I love it," I confirmed, answering honestly. "It's got to be so nice for you to know after a week of being in the craziness of the city that you've got this waiting for you."

"You don't enjoy being in the city?"

My hand stroked over his torso. "I do. I actually really do love it. But it's not a place I plan to spend the rest of my life. One day, when I'm ready to have a family, I don't want to be in all the madness there. I'd like knowing I was close enough to get there whenever I wanted to visit, but far enough away that I could have this kind of peace."

Ben didn't respond, and the silence stretched between us again.

That's when I knew I had to tell him. I pressed my palm into his chest, sat up, and looked him in the eyes.

When I had his attention, I said softly, "You know I love you, too, right?"

Ben's hand came up and cupped my cheek. As his thumb stroked back and forth, he assured me, "I know."

"How?" I wondered.

"If you didn't, they never would have captured you crying," he reasoned. He gave himself a moment to compose himself before he went on, "I hope you know just how sorry I am about that, Cora. It broke my heart to see you cry."

I leaned into his touch and closed my eyes. Feeling his gentle caress of my skin, I whispered, "I know."

"Do you?" he asked.

I nodded.

Ben's eyes searched my face as if trying to assess whether or not I was being honest. I assumed he found what he was looking for because his hand that had been cupping my cheek left my face as he put his arm around my shoulder to curl me into his chest again.

Once I was there, he gave me a gentle squeeze and stated, "I was wrong."

"What?" I returned, pressing my palm to his chest again so I could push back to look at him.

"You're the first woman I've gotten serious with like this, Cora," he began. "I'm new at this. And I might not always make the best choices. But I can promise you that I would never intentionally set out to hurt you."

"I appreciate what you're saying, Ben, but I don't understand. What were you wrong about?" I pressed.

"Lisa," he told me. My body instantly froze. Ben noticed and quickly explained, "It didn't dawn on me when I took her in my car to the lunch meeting that it was something that could hurt you. From my perspective, it was a business meeting… something I've done hundreds of times with many clients over the years. So, this was no different. Like I said, I haven't done the serious relationship thing, so I never thought about it. But I want you to know that I have a mind to it now, and I won't do that again."

"Ben, you don't have to—" I got out before he cut me off.

"I do, baby," he insisted. "Your feelings are important to me. I hurt you because I did what I did. It wasn't intentional, but it still happened. That's not going to happen again. From this point forward, female clients will not be riding in my car to a business lunch. It's disrespectful to you."

I couldn't believe he was for real. Ben was going to change the way he conducted business meetings out of respect for me. I hadn't expected him to do that, nor would I have asked him, but the fact that he did spoke volumes about just the kind of man he was.

"So, what's happening with Lisa now?" I wondered.

"What do you mean?"

I hesitated to respond. I wanted to know if she was going to be someone I'd need to constantly worry about hitting on Ben, but I didn't want him thinking that I was the crazy girlfriend. Finally, I blurted, "I assume she's still your client."

Ben nodded. "Yes, but she's going to be making arrangements to move back to New Hampshire to be with her mom for the foreseeable future. Given her upcoming divorce, she needs to get away. After I made it clear that I wasn't okay with what she tried to do considering I'm happy in my current relationship, she apologized profusely. She was mortified. I think she's just hurting over a lot of things and wanted comfort. Unfortunately, I'm not that man for her. So, I'll still have her on as a client, but there's nothing more beyond that. And I don't think I'll have much one-on-one interaction with her over the coming months anyway."

I nodded my understanding.

Ben added, "But I want you to know that if, when I do have to meet with her, she ever tries what she did today again, I'll be cutting ties with her. Not only is it unprofessional, it'll then also be disrespectful. I can give her the benefit of the doubt of not knowing my personal relationship status this time. I can't do that a second time."

A smile spread across my face. "I love you," I whispered.

"I love you, too," he replied.

Slipping my arms back around his torso, I cuddled my body into his again. Ben kept one of his arms wrapped around my back and the other draped across my thighs.

We stayed like that for a long while without any words. Eventually, though, I wanted to switch gears. So, I asked, "Am I invited to Christmas?"

Without any hesitation, Ben replied, "If you're not going, I'm not going."

I let out a laugh. "You don't mean that."

"I do," he assured me. "I want you there. Besides, even though I'm going to introduce you to Mom and Dad well before then, Will and Ash won't be here until Christmas."

He wanted me to meet his parents. I loved that he wanted that. And because he did, I blurted, "I'll come to Christmas with your family if you come to Thanksgiving with mine in two weeks."

"Works for me," he agreed. "But I want you to myself on the last day of the year."

That was a fair and reasonable compromise. Truthfully, I didn't think it was a hardship in the slightest, especially if he brought me here.

"New Year's Eve in Rosewood?" I purred. "I think that sounds fabulous."

"You mean you don't want to stay in the city for that?" he asked.

I tipped my head back to look up at him. "Do you?" I returned, a bit shocked that he would want to stay there.

Ben's lips twitched as he fought the grin from breaking out across his face. That's when I realized he was teasing me.

I simply shook my head at him and cuddled back into his body.

"When I woke up this morning, I didn't think I'd be here planning my holidays with you," I noted a few minutes later.

"Cora…" He trailed off as his hand tightened on my shoulder. "Baby, I'm so sorry."

My arms instinctively squeezed him. "I know. I'm not looking for another apology, Ben. I just think it's funny how you managed to get me to change my whole perspective. It hasn't even been a full twenty-four hours and here I am in your arms again. This doesn't bode well for my future. Clearly, I can't put up a fight."

"Are you serious?" he countered. "You had no problem basically walking right by me and into your apartment. You barely said two words to me."

"I wanted to throw myself into your arms and hug you, though. My heart hurt more just hearing the pain in your voice, and it took superhuman effort to stick to my guns," I explained. After a few seconds passed, I apologized, "I'm sorry I didn't give you a fair chance to explain right then."

Ben pressed a kiss to the top of my head. "It's okay. You had every reason to react the way you did. I'm not upset with you at all."

"I think we're both playing the part of remorseful lovers right now. Perhaps we should find a way to make it up to one another," I suggested.

There was a chill in the air, but I hadn't noticed it since I was cuddled close to Ben under a blanket while we sat beside the fire. But at my words, his hand that had been draped across my thighs slid up them and toward my hip until it stopped at the hem of my shirt. And when his fingers lifted it and brushed against my skin, a shiver ran through me.

"Got any ideas on how we could do that for each other?" he asked when my eyes met his.

His fingers continued to move along my skin up the front of my body. He cupped my breast in his hand and waited for me to respond.

Hoping he could see the twinkle in my eyes, I smiled and reasoned, "I think you've already figured that out."

Ben dropped his mouth to mine and gave me a soft kiss on the lips. I pulled back just a touch and whispered against them, "Make love to me right here by the fire, Ben."

He smiled against my lips and kissed me again.

Then, Ben and I spent the next few hours proving to one another just how sorry we were for what we'd done to one another.

CHAPTER 13

Cora

BEN'S WARM BODY CURLED AROUND THE BACK OF MINE AS one of his hands came to my hip. His other hand brushed my hair over my shoulder, and he nuzzled his face in my neck.

Even though I was in the middle of something, I was easily distracted by him. Leaning back into him, I tipped my head to the opposite side and gave him unhindered access to my neck. I was not disappointed.

Because Ben began trailing his lips lightly over my skin there.

"Mmm," I hummed, arching my back.

The grip Ben had on my hip tightened. He continued to move his mouth along the side of my throat for a moment before moving to my jaw. When he made it to the side of my head, he inhaled deeply and whispered, "I thought we were sleeping in this morning."

I stifled a laugh and noted, "We did. I did. But it started getting late, and I had a few things I needed to do still."

Ben's head pulled back from mine, and I watched as he turned to look at the clock on the microwave. "It's nine-thirty," he stated.

"Yeah?"

"That's not late," he insisted.

With a smile tugging at my lips, I pointed out, "Any other day you would have already been up for at least three hours by now."

Ben buried his face in my neck again as his hand that had been at my hip slid under his t-shirt I was wearing and moved up the side of my body until he cupped my breast. My head dropped back against his shoulder. I didn't continue to give him unhindered access to my throat, though. Instead, I turned my gaze in his direction where he wasted no time in touching his mouth to mine.

When he pulled back to look down at me, he smiled and admitted, "You're right, but this isn't any other day. This is the morning after we decided we'd sleep in."

"I did sleep in," I maintained. "I've only been down here for about an hour."

"Baby, sleeping in means we wake up together and make love before we start the day," Ben told me.

"Ben, you woke me up before the sun even rose this morning and made love to me," I reminded him.

His fingers worked my breast, his thumb moving back and forth over my nipple, while his other hand began trailing down the front of my body. I could feel him hard behind me, his erection pressing into my ass.

Suffice it to say that Ben had no shortage of appreciation or interest in me.

"Are you saying that was enough for you?" he asked as his hand dipped lower and cupped me between the legs.

What was I supposed to say to that?

"I'm not sure how to answer that," I started. "Either way, it can be held against me. If it wasn't enough, you'll think you're falling down on the job. If it was enough, you'll think I've had my fill of you. And neither of those assumptions could be further from the truth. I always want more of you, Ben. Always. That's simply because when you do give it to me, it's beyond measure how good it is."

With another flick of his thumb over my nipple, he shared, "I was hoping for a brief respite before I had you again. I thought we were simply resting up after the early morning session."

I was trying to stay focused on what I was doing, but Ben's hands were doing so many wonderfully delicious things to my body that I was finding it difficult to concentrate. Pressing one of my palms into the countertop, I brought the other hand up to my mouth. Closing my mouth around my forefinger, I began sucking and licking it.

Instantly, Ben's body tensed behind mine. His grip on my breast tightened and his hand between my legs stilled. I cocked an eyebrow and shot him my most seductive look. Sliding my finger from between my lips, I watched Ben's gaze grow heated.

"What are you doing?" he whispered, but the fascination in his tone was unmistakable.

I leaned toward him and kissed him. My tongue swept into his mouth.

Ben groaned.

I let him taste me for a bit before I pulled back and smiled at him.

"Why do you taste like chocolate?" he asked.

Then, his eyes went to the island and widened.

Ben didn't say anything about what he saw, so I declared, "I know this is supposed to be our week off together because of the holidays, but I figured this wasn't really work. Besides, we'll both be able to enjoy this later anyway."

He raised his brows. "Enjoy it?" he semi-repeated.

I bit my lip in an attempt to not burst out laughing. When I thought I had it under control, I answered, "Yes."

Ben took a step back, his hands leaving the most intimate parts of my body. "Cora, baby, you're asking me to eat a dick," he stressed.

"A chocolate one!" I cried. "It's not real!"

Ben simply stared at me.

"I'll give you one of the little ones," I reasoned. "Surely you can handle two inches. It's not a big deal. I need help deciding what the best option is."

"I'll give my input," he assured me. "But I don't need to eat it to do that."

I rolled my eyes and shook my head. "You're being ridiculous. I'll just have Ash help me when she and Will get here later this afternoon."

"That might be a wise idea," he started. "But I promise I'll help you out with making a decision on the aesthetics."

"Fine," I huffed, looking back at the mess I had made of the island. There were chocolate molds waiting to be filled, a plate covered in already-made tiny chocolate penises, and only one of the large ones. It took a bit longer for those to set and required substantially more chocolate.

I filled up the last three spots in the final mold I had and moved it to the refrigerator. When I stood up and looked at Ben, I asked, "Did I ruin your morning?"

His brows pulled together. "Over this?" he asked.

"No, Ben. Did I ruin your morning because I wasn't in bed with you this morning when you woke up?" I clarified.

His face softened as he stepped toward me. Bringing a hand up to tuck a strand of my hair behind my ear, he said, "I would have liked to have you in bed with me this morning, but that doesn't mean we can't make up for it. Besides, it's technically still morning. I think we can turn it around."

Suddenly, I had an idea. "How do you feel about melted chocolate and me for breakfast?" I teased.

Ben tilted his head to this side, cocked an eyebrow, and thought a moment. Then, he decided, "Yeah, I think that'll work."

At that, I curled my fingers around the hem of Ben's shirt I had on and whipped it over my head. Then, I shoved my hands in the side of my panties at my hips and pushed them down my legs. Ben quickly removed his boxer briefs as I walked toward him.

Seconds later, I realized Ben didn't have an affliction

for chocolate. He liked it just fine. But he seemed to prefer it when he was licking it off my body as a means to turn around the fact that he'd woken up without me beside him in bed.

Quite some time later, Ben and I were a mess of tangled bodies on the kitchen floor. I had suspected there'd be a mess to clean up considering the use of chocolate, but there wasn't. Apparently, we were both sure not to waste much of it.

"We're sticky," I declared, my body mostly on top of Ben's as he kept an arm wrapped around my back.

"Yeah," he agreed.

"We have to get up and get in the shower to clean ourselves up. Will and Ash are going to be here soon."

"They aren't coming until lunchtime," Ben reasoned.

"I know, but we're going to end up in the shower," I noted. "Don't act like you're going to behave if we go in there together."

He chuckled. "Point made."

Ben and I stayed there a touch longer, allowing our breath to return to normal. A few minutes of silence later, we peeled ourselves off the floor and made our way to the shower. As I had suspected, Ben didn't behave himself.

It was a few hours after Ben found me in the kitchen and successfully managed to seduce me. Will and Ash were going to be coming over to visit us. I met the both of them two days ago when I joined Ben and his family for Christmas at his parents' house and immediately fell in love with them.

Ash and I hit it off. Will was great, too. Best of all, I loved seeing Ben around his family. It was clear that he and his brother were extremely close.

On Christmas night, when we got back to Ben's place, I talked to him about it.

"You miss him," I stated.

"What?"

"Your brother," I clarified. "It's clear to me that you miss him terribly."

There was a moment of hesitation before he confirmed, "Yeah. We were really close growing up. I know he's happy doing what he's doing, but it's tough not having him around. He's been traveling for so long, I thought I would be used to it by now, but it doesn't seem to have gotten any easier."

My heart hurt for him. "I'm sorry," I lamented. "Do you think he'll always travel like this?"

Ben took in a deep breath. "Probably," he sighed. "It's his livelihood. And he and Ash love getting to see the world."

"Wow," I murmured. "I don't know what to say. At least you guys seem to be able to pick right back up where you left off when he comes home to visit. And you get to video chat with him."

"Yeah," Ben agreed.

Noticing his despondency over the subject, I decided

it was best to let it go. Even still, I hated that he was upset. So, that night, I had suggested to Ben that he try to spend as much time as possible with his brother while he was here. He agreed to it, but also wanted me there. Ash was going to be with her husband, so having another woman around would make it better for her, too.

And that's why I was here now.

Well, it was part of the reason anyway.

The truth was that things between Ben and I had been going great for the last month or so. After the whole situation went down with Lisa and the tabloids, Ben had been working overtime to make up for the fact that I'd been hurt. While I appreciated the effort he was making to do that, it really wasn't necessary anymore.

And that all came down to a few words he had said to me that night we worked things out. Either I trusted him or I didn't. No amount of love he had for me would be able to change that. Ever since he'd said that, I realized just how important it was that I started looking at things that way.

Sure, I could have allowed the insecurities I had from my previous relationship to be my excuse. I could have told Ben that I wasn't sure I could trust him. But that wasn't what I wanted. That wasn't who I wanted to be. Other than that incident, Ben had done nothing to earn my distrust other than come after the guy who had left me scorned.

So, I took the time over the days that followed after we'd made up with one another to really think about how everything surrounding that situation had happened. And while it was easy to see that I had a justifiable reason to be upset about what I saw, it didn't mean I handled it the best way.

Knowing what I did about Ben and the way he made me feel, I should have done something other than what I did. When he realized the reason why I hadn't answered or returned his calls, he put in the effort to save us. He was worried sick about me. I knew that the minute I heard his voice when I got off that elevator.

What did I do? I ran down the street and turned my phone off so he couldn't contact me.

So, I took a long, hard look at myself and my actions. I looked at Ben and his actions. And in doing that I learned that it was easy for me to lump him in a category with my ex because I was scared. But when it came down to it, Ben was the real deal.

He wasn't just some rich guy who was a jerk because he could be one. Things were important to him. People were important to him. *We* were important to him.

Ben proved himself and his love to me. He proved his faithfulness. And he made it very clear to me that he wasn't just some guy who wanted to play the part when it suited him. He was all in with me. So, I let it all go. I let go of my fears and worries and insecurities.

There was no longer any reason to have them.

Because even though Ben and I had only been together for just under three months, he'd shown me what a real relationship was supposed to be like. For someone who claimed he hadn't ever been in a long-standing relationship before the one he had with me, Ben seemed to know just what to do in any situation. The integrity of our relationship was of the utmost importance to him.

I had no doubts about where I stood in his life.

And that's why I was here now, two days after Christmas, staying with Ben at his place in Rosewood. We had been able to spend the entire week with one another since Ben wasn't going back into his office until after the holidays. He did have a few moments over the last week where he put in hours from home, but I barely noticed it. Typically, his work schedule meant that he didn't get much uninterrupted time off, so this was a really nice change of pace for the both of us.

Our plan was to spend the day with his brother and sister-in-law before they took off on their next adventure. I didn't know when the two of them would be back for their next visit, but I hoped it wouldn't be too long. The truth was, not only did Ben miss his brother terribly when he was gone, but I found that I really liked them both. If things continued to go well between Ben and me, I thought it would be nice for us to have a couple with which to go on the occasional double date.

I was currently back in the kitchen. Following our love-making session in the shower, we came out and cleaned up the mess we'd left behind. Then, I got started on preparing our lunch. Ben helped out by pulling ingredients I needed out from the fridge, but otherwise, he simply kept me company.

When the doorbell rang, Ben stood and declared, "I'll get it."

"Okay," I called to his departing backside as he walked out of the kitchen.

A minute later, Ash's voice filled the room. "It smells great in here. What are you making?"

I glanced over at her from where I was standing at the stove and answered, "I just pulled the bacon out of the oven a few minutes ago, so that's probably what you're smelling right now."

"Bacon?" Will repeated.

Nodding, I explained, "I checked with Ben ahead of time to make sure nobody had any food issues. I'm going to chop up the bacon so we can use it as a topping for my creamy potato soup. It's just about ready. And while I was waiting for the potatoes to finish cooking, I made the chicken and bacon sandwiches."

"That sounds amazing," Ash declared.

Will glanced in his brother's direction and gave him a look of approval. I'd seen him give Ben that same look on Christmas Day when Ben introduced me to them.

"Do you need any help, baby?" Ben asked.

"You two go away and do some brotherly bonding," Ash ordered. "I'll help Cora out here."

With that, the men walked away and left Ash and me alone.

I had added the final ingredients to the soup and was simply stirring it to break down the potatoes when she asked, "Okay, what can I do?"

"I've got a baguette over there that needs to be sliced if you don't mind," I replied, jerking my head toward the opposite counter.

"Not at all," she insisted, moving to it. "It's the least I could do considering you're hosting us."

I let out a laugh and noted, "Well, Ben's technically doing the hosting. I'm just making the food."

Ash got to work on slicing the baguette and promised, "You are not, and you know it."

I had to admit it felt good to hear that. I smiled at her and said, "Thanks."

"So, now are you booked with weddings after the holidays or…" She trailed off.

Shaking my head, I replied, "Not at all. This isn't wedding season, so it's typically pretty slow at this time of year. My next wedding isn't until February. But I'm keeping myself busy preparing for the bachelorette party."

Ash stopped slicing as her eyes shot to mine. "You get to go to the bachelorette parties?" she asked.

"No," I answered through my laughter. "I mean, I've been invited on more than one occasion, but I don't go. It's one of the rules that I have. Of course, I had a rule about never actually being in the wedding, and that was shot to smithereens."

"Yeah, but look at the bright side," she encouraged me. "Now you and Ben are together. Can you imagine if Priscilla had gotten someone else to fill in instead of you? I doubt I'd be here right now slicing a baguette."

The thought that someone else could be here with Ben instead of me made my head spin, so as fast as it came into my mind, I pushed it out.

My thoughts must have been written all over my

face because Ash murmured, "I see that just hit some-where deep."

"It's not a good thought," I confirmed. "Anyway, I made an exception one time, and it all turned out great in the end. And it's precisely the reason why I don't need to go to any bachelorette parties now. I simply do all of the planning and come up with the ideas."

"But you're missing out on all the fun," she argued.

I turned off the stove, moved the soup from the heat, and walked to the refrigerator. When I stuck my head inside to get something out, I corrected her. "Actually, I think I get to have a ton of fun."

Seconds later, I set a tray of tiny penises down on the island counter in front of where she was working.

Ash's face lit up and her eyes widened. "What are you doing with those?"

"Planning a bachelorette party for the February wed-ding," I replied, walking back to the refrigerator. "I'm trying to figure out what makes more sense. Those…" I trailed off as I pulled out the other surprise. "Or this," I stated as I held up the eight-inch one.

"Wow," she marveled. "That's a lot of chocolate."

A grin spread across my face as I nodded at her. "That's why I'm leaning toward the little ones. The big one is nice, but who is realistically going to eat this much chocolate in one sitting?"

Her gaze went to the plate on the island. "These ones are so cute. I hope you won't mind sharing one after lunch."

"I was hoping you'd be up for it," I started. "I tried talking Ben into it this morning, but he refused."

She rolled her eyes. "That doesn't surprise me; Will would be the same way."

"If I didn't think they'd go crazy about it, I'd say we should put them in the middle of the table during lunch," I suggested.

"Yes!" she exclaimed, clearly in agreement with my idea. "But it'll be too much of a distraction. It's probably better to wait until afterward."

"Yeah, you're right," I agreed.

With that, Ash and I got the soup ladled into the bowls and set out on the table. I pulled the sandwiches from the oven where I'd left them to keep them warm and toasty. Then, we called out the men and ate lunch.

"The food was great, Cora," Ben praised, leaning toward me.

"Thanks," I returned. "I'm glad you enjoyed it."

"There was bacon, Ben," Will chimed in. "Bacon makes everything better."

With my eyes still on Ben's, I tipped my head in Will's direction and noted, "He's got a point."

"Of course, that does not mean that I think this would have been bad without the bacon," Will added, bringing his eyes to me. "In case you were worried."

I let out a laugh. "Not at all."

From the moment we sat down to eat, the four of us had a great time visiting with one another. I loved being able to see Ben interact with his family and appreciated the fact that they made me feel like I belonged there with them.

When we'd all had our fill, I looked to Will and Ash and asked, "So, where are you two off to next?"

"The Maldives," Ash answered. "I'm so excited to go."

"Oh, wow," I marveled. "I've heard it's beautiful there. Is this your first time visiting?"

Will and Ash both nodded, but Will responded, "Yes. And we're so glad we picked it when we did. The weather is perfect there at this time of year, so it'll be an amazing trip."

"How long are you staying there?" Ben asked.

"Only a week and a half," Ash offered.

Ben seemed surprised by that because he pressed, "Really? Isn't that a bit short for the two of you? Where are you going afterward?"

Ash and Will looked at one another before turning their attention back to Ben and me. Will's eyes settled on his brother before he shared, "Yes, it is short. But we're planning to splurge while we're there and get one of the water villas. Afterward, we've decided to change things up and do a bit of driving."

My brows pulled together as Ben asked, "What?"

Excitedly, Ash exclaimed, "We're coming back to the U.S. and going to do a few road trips over the next couple of months!"

I watched as Ben sat back in his seat and narrowed his eyes. Something wasn't sitting right with him. If I hadn't seen the look on Ben's face, I never would have thought twice about their plans. But seeing that look combined with the one I saw on Will's face, I knew something was up.

Ashley turned her head toward her husband and leaned into him. That's when Will shared, "Ash and I have decided to move back to Rosewood. We want to travel domestically for a while."

"Why?" Ben wondered.

Putting his arm around his wife's shoulders and curling her into his body, Will replied, "Because we recently found out that Ash is pregnant, and we want to have a home base for the duration of the pregnancy."

Wow.

Wow.

This was fantastic news.

Ben's brother and sister-in-law were pregnant and moving home. Ben was going to have his brother back. At least for the foreseeable future.

"Are you serious?" Ben asked, his voice sounding strained.

Will nodded.

Ben held his brother's eyes briefly before he pushed his chair back from the table and stood. As Ben moved around the table toward his brother, Will stood.

Then, I witnessed the most beautiful thing as Ben threw his arms around Will and pulled him into a hug. "Fuck, it's going to be good to have you home," he told him. "Congratulations on the baby."

"Thanks, Ben. We're really excited."

Ben stepped back, moved to Ashley, and gave her a hug and a kiss on the cheek. "Congratulations, Ash."

"Thank you," she returned.

By the time he stepped back, I had rounded the table to congratulate the both of them. "This is so exciting," I bubbled before pulling each of them into a hug and offering congratulatory words.

When I stepped back, Ben had wrapped his arm around me and tugged me close to him. When I tipped my head back to look at him, I could see just how happy he was.

I didn't get a chance to say anything to him, though, because Ash declared, "I think we need some celebratory chocolate!"

"Yes!" I cried. "I'll go get it."

Ben groaned as Will asked, "What chocolate?"

I didn't wait around for the explanation as I dashed off to the kitchen to grab dessert.

"Are you excited?" I asked Ben.

It was hours after Will and Ash left, and Ben and I had just made love to one another. We were curled up together in his bed, my body resting half on his with my cheek pressed to his chest.

"About what?" he asked.

"Becoming an uncle," I clarified.

Ben took a moment to respond, but when he did, I could hear the contentment in his tone. "Yeah," he sighed.

"I can't wait. And I'm really happy about Will and Ash coming back home."

Lifting my head, I rested my chin on his chest and questioned him. "Do you think they'll stay here after the baby is born?"

"I don't know. I hope they do."

Smiling at him, I said, "I hope they do, too. They're so much fun to be around."

Ben's arm tightened around me. "Do you want kids one day?" he asked.

"Not yet. But one day I'd like kids."

"How many?"

"One or two," I confirmed.

Ben's body relaxed as he sighed.

I wasn't sure what that meant, so I asked, "Is that... are you... how many do you want?"

"I could be happy with one or two," he told me.

Wondering if he was looking for this to happen sometime soon, I questioned him, "You aren't looking to have kids right now, are you?"

Ben let out a laugh. "Cora, we haven't even been together for three months yet. I know I'm a catch and all, but we can slow it down a little," he teased.

I lifted my chin from his chest and argued, "You're the one who brought it up."

"I know, but I want to marry you first."

My breath stuck in my throat. I swallowed hard and stared at him. Ben held my gaze, realized I was freaking out, and gave me a shake. "Relax, baby," he ordered. "That wasn't a proposal."

I did as he asked and let the breath rush past my lips.

"That wasn't the reaction I was expecting," he mumbled.

"I'm sorry, Ben. You caught me off guard. I wasn't expecting the conversation to take that turn," I noted.

"What if I had asked?" he wondered.

"To marry you?"

He dipped his chin.

What would I have done if Ben asked me to marry him? As he had just said, we hadn't even been together for three months. And I knew that there were people who had marriages that could stand the test of time despite their short courtship. I just never thought that I would be one of them.

But I'd also been in a long-term relationship with someone I thought I was going to marry. That man proved to be anything but right for me.

So, this wasn't about the length of time I was in a relationship. It all came down to the individual. It was about being with someone who wasn't just playing a part for the sake of it. It was about someone who wanted to fulfill a role that was important to them.

And I knew Ben was that man for me.

Instead of giving him the answer he was looking for, I cocked an eyebrow and teased, "I guess we'll have to wait and see when you ask."

With that, Ben tightened his arms around me, rolled us so I was on my back, and promised, "Let's hope you're prepared for that when it happens."

I loved that he said that with such conviction.

When it happens.

I couldn't wait.

And because it meant so much to me, I lifted my head and touched my mouth to his. Ben didn't hesitate to commence another round of lovemaking.

EPILOGUE

Ben
Ten months later

"OKAY, ARE YOU READY FOR THIS?" CORA ASKED THE minute I walked from the bathroom following my shower and into the bedroom.

She was sitting at the head of our bed nestled between the pillows, her back against the headboard. Her knees were bent and pulled up toward her chest. I had no idea what she was asking me about. All I knew was that she was the most beautiful woman in the world.

And she was all mine.

"I don't know. What?" I returned.

Cora dropped her gaze to her thighs, and I grew concerned that something was wrong.

But before I had the chance to say anything, she said, "Confirmed. Benjamin Mason has made it official."

Cora's eyes came to mine. She smiled brightly before focusing her attention at her thighs again.

"Rumors started swirling four months ago when the finance mogul's long-time girlfriend, Cora Daniels, was spotted wearing a ring. While an official engagement announcement wasn't made, it was hard to view the ring as anything but one that indicated a wedding was on the horizon."

Cora paused as I moved and sat down next to her on the bed. That's when I saw the tabloid sitting in her lap. She leaned toward me and kissed me before she continued reading.

"Three days ago, the pair were spotted at John F. Kennedy International Airport. While their tans indicated they'd traipsed off to some tropical location, it was the solid band on Mason's left hand, pictured below, that confirmed the rumors."

I shook my head and chuckled. It amazed me that my relationship status was of such interest to the reporters. Even still, they weren't wrong about what had happened.

A few months ago, I had proposed to Cora. She accepted my proposal, and the two of us spent all of five minutes discussing how we planned to get married. The meaning behind getting married was what was important to us. The frills weren't.

So, we decided on a destination wedding.

Cora and I got our families and her best friend on board and flew to Fiji. It was a small gathering, but it was perfect.

Nearly as perfect as her.

"At least they waited until they were absolutely certain to run anything," I reasoned.

Cora leaned her shoulder into mine. "I never thought

I could feel this happy," she told me. "You've changed my life."

Wrapping an arm around her back to her opposite shoulder, I gave her a squeeze, pressed a kiss to her temple, and whispered, "You did the same for me, baby."

That was the truth.

Never in a million years did I think things would work out for me the way they did. I didn't doubt that I'd eventually be able to find someone to spend my life with, but I never thought I'd get so lucky to meet her the moment I set out to find her.

Yet, somehow, I did.

And to this day I can't help but feel immensely grateful. For her and the chance to love her.

"I don't know if I'll ever get used to it," she returned, her voice soft. "But honestly, I'm not sure if I want to."

"I understand exactly what you mean. It's been just over a year now since we met and every day has just gotten better than the last. Even our wedding," I told her.

"Our wedding?" she repeated.

Nodding, I explained, "I never thought it would be possible to top that day. I mean, we shouldn't be able to, right? That's supposed to be the most magical day of our lives. But you've already managed to do that for me."

Cora tipped her head back and looked up at me. "I have?"

"Yeah. Today. Just walking out of the bathroom after taking a shower and seeing you sitting here in the middle of our bed was enough. I look at you, realize you're all mine, and there's nothing that can top that. So, I figure, every day that I get to look at you is going to be the best day of my life."

She smiled and cocked an eyebrow at me. "Until someone else comes along."

Cora seemed to be teasing me, but I couldn't understand why she'd ever joke about something like that. "Excuse me?"

"Not quite a year ago you told me you wanted to marry me before you made a baby with me," she started. Then, she shrugged her shoulders before she continued, "We're married now."

I eyed her curiously. "You're not—"

"I'm not," she cut me off. "But I wouldn't mind trying if you think it's something you're ready for."

I had been ready. For a long time.

And once my nephew was born a couple months ago, I found myself thinking about it more frequently. Perhaps Cora had been feeling the same.

"Really?" I asked.

She nodded slowly as a smile spread across her face.

I reached my hand over and took the tabloid off her legs. After tossing it to the floor, I shifted my wife's body in the bed and settled myself over her. "Do you want to start practicing tonight?" I asked.

Cora framed my face in her hands and searched my face. After several moments of silence, she said, "The day Priscilla got married, I was dreading having to be paired up with you. I didn't think my heart could handle a man like you. But then you showed me that you weren't the guy I presumed you to be. And while you initially did what you had to do and played the part of my fake boy-friend just to get a date with me, I quickly realized there was so much more to you. You stole my heart in a matter of days, Ben. You became an amazing boyfriend. Then, you filled the role as my fiancé before you became my husband. These last few weeks have been nothing short of amazing, and you've given me so much. Yet, some-how, I'm still feeling greedy. I want to see you as a father to our baby."

I couldn't handle all that she was saying to me. I had no idea how to respond to it all. Thankfully, I didn't have to because Cora continued, "So yes, Ben, I want to start now. I want us to be parents because while I have no doubts in my mind about the kind of father you'll be, I still want to see it with my eyes."

"I love you, Cora."

She lifted her head, touched her lips to mine, and whispered, "I love you, too."

When I made no move to do anything, she de-manded, "Kiss me and practice making a baby with me."

I smiled against her lips, but then I did as she asked.

ACKNOWLEDGEMENTS

To my husband, Jeff—Always. I'll always be grateful for you and all that you do. Thank you for being on this journey through life with me. There's nobody else I'd rather do it with than you. I love you.

To my boys, J&J—The lights of my life… even when you make me crazy. Thank you for constantly finding ways to surprise me. I hope you always go after what you want in life. Mommy and Daddy will be there to support you every step of the way.

To my loyal readers—Thank you hardly seems like enough. But it's all I've got. That and more stories. This has been an incredible journey so far. I hope you'll stay until the end.

To S.H., S.B., & E.M.—As always, thank you for making my books shine. You're all brilliant.

To the bloggers—It's impossible to convey just how much your effort and support for my words means to me. Thank you… from the bottom of my heart, thank you so much.

CONNECT WITH
A.K. EVANS

To stay connected with A.K. Evans and receive all the first looks at upcoming releases, latest news, or to simply follow along on her journey, be sure to add or follow her on social media. You can also get the scoop by signing up for the monthly newsletter, which includes a giveaway every month.

Newsletter: http://eepurl.com/dmeo6z

Website: www.authorakevans.com

Facebook: www.facebook.com/authorAKEvans

Facebook Reader Group: www.facebook.com/
groups/1285069088272037

Instagram: www.instagram.com/authorakevans

Twitter: twitter.com/AuthorAKEvans

Goodreads Author Page: www.goodreads.com/user/
show/64525877-a-k-evans

Subscribe on YouTube: http://bit.ly2w01yb7

Twitter: twitter.com/AuthorAKEvans

OTHER BOOKS BY
A.K. EVANS

The Everything Series
Everything I Need
Everything I Have
Everything I Want
Everything I Love

The Cunningham Security Series
Obsessed
Overcome
Desperate
Solitude
Burned
Unworthy
Surrender

Betrayed (Coming February 11, 2020)
Revived (Coming June 16, 2020)

Road Trip Romance
Tip the Scales
Play the Part

One Wrong Turn (Coming January 7, 2020)
Just a Fling (Coming March 2020)

ABOUT
A.K. EVANS

A.K. Evans is a married mother of two boys residing in a small town in northeastern Pennsylvania, where she graduated from Lafayette College in 2004 with two degrees (one in English and one in Economics & Business). Following a brief stint in the insurance and financial services industry, Evans realized the career was not for her and went on to manage her husband's performance automotive business. She even drove the shop's race cars! Looking for more personal fulfillment after eleven years in the automotive industry, Andrea decided to pursue her dream of becoming a writer.

While Andrea continues to help administratively with her husband's businesses, she spends most of her time writing and homeschooling her two boys. When she finds scraps of spare time, Evans enjoys reading, doing yoga, watching NY Rangers hockey, dancing, and vacationing with her family. Andrea, her husband, and her children are currently working on taking road trips to visit all 50 states (though, Alaska and Hawaii might require flights).

Made in the USA
Middletown, DE
01 July 2022

68269992R00116